GW00888895

Also by James Litherland

The Slowpocalypse Series

Certain Hypothetical
Threat Multiplication
Compromised Inside
Peripheral Encounters
Political Homicide

The Watchbearers Series

Millennium Crash
Centenary Separation
Uncertain Murder
Prohibited Activities
Temporal Entanglement

The Miraibanashi Series

Whispers of the Dead
Enemies of the Batsu
Endurance of the Free

For more information, please visit
www.OutpostStories.com

SEISMIC DISRUPTION

DEDICATION

To God be the Glory

(and all criticism should be directed at the author.)

SEISMIC DISRUPTION

JAMES LITHERLAND

Outpost Stories

Disclaimer: As should be obvious, this book is a complete work of fiction. Any resemblance to real persons, places, or things is entirely coincidental.

ISBN 13: 978-1-946273-22-2

Cover design by James Litherland

The Slowpocalypse

AS SOCIETY SLOWLY started falling apart, lawyer Jonathan Miles designed a massive government project—several secure, federally-run facilities, integrated university and research complexes with their own self-sustaining communities—and he concealed within those plans a scheme to use the compounds as arks to weather the approaching collapse of civilization. And he was made the director of the first to be finished, in Central Florida.

Events forced him to seal that FURC before the time had come, to protect the community from those who wanted the facilities for themselves. And courageous men and women successfully defended the compound against a series of threats from within as well as from outside their walls. Finally achieving a measure of calm and safety, the residents have spent three years trying to build a new society and preparing to rebuild the world out of the ashes of the old.

But the plans of men get swept away by the acts of God...

Contents

Part One: Immediate Reactions

Part Two: Committed Action

Part One

Immediate Reactions

Chapter 1

Careful What You Wish

9:35 p.m. Friday, May 27th
The rooftop of Cameron's Luxury Suites

KAT LEANED BACK into Tony and sighed with contentment as she gazed up at the night sky. Here in what some called the warehouse district, the relative lack of lights made it possible to appreciate the full panoply of stars overhead. An appropriately romantic view. The air was pleasantly warm, and the soft, cool breeze blew a hint of salty tang in from the ocean. Or seemed to.

Since the Gulf was roughly sixty miles west and the Atlantic about fifty to the east, it was likely just her imagination. If only she could use that power to put them on the gently swaying deck of a boat out on the water, waves lapping against the hull...

Tony's cheek rested against the side of her head, and the muscles of his mouth moved—she felt it and knew he'd smiled. "Still no regrets?" And though it sounded teasing, his tone still questioned.

A slight shake of her head should be enough of a response. Their third anniversary and the man still doubted she could be satisfied with him as her husband. And after all she'd done just in the past hour to show him how she felt.

It was the age difference, of course, among other things—like her father being Tony's closest friend since she'd been a little girl. "My only regret is that it took mother's interference to force your hand."

Now he sighed, the familiar expression of exasperation whenever Caroline came into their conversation. After her initial outrage, Kat could now only be grateful for what her mom had done, though she avoided admitting as much to the woman, still used it against her when they argued.

"Let's leave Care out of this. We're supposed to be enjoying ourselves."

Kat grinned. "And you haven't been?"

This place was where he'd brought her for their rather belated honeymoon. A gift from Ken to them both. Though 'Cameron's Luxury Suites', as he had eventually named it, was now a popular getaway for FURC residents, if an expensive one. He'd converted an emptied warehouse into this two-story hotel—

eight large luxury suites with all the amenities. And a long waiting list.

Whether it was her being his deputy or her husband being an old friend, Ken had given them a full week in one of the suites for their honeymoon. And a couple nights for every anniversary after. So Sunday they'd return home, and Monday would see the two of them back at work. Separately.

Strange to think that holing up in a hotel room, when they were all shut away from the world behind walls and fences and guards, would be considered a retreat. But if people couldn't leave the compound, this was the closest they could come to escaping the reality of their situation. And people needed breaks and holidays.

She, for one, also needed adventure. And while she'd thought she'd had enough excitement to last a lifetime three years ago, the past thirty-odd months of relative calm had cured her of that notion. Every now and then an infected individual or small group of thugs would attack, try to enter the compound by force, but nothing her guards couldn't handle. And Tony's security officers still had troublemakers that needed dealing with. The Lift Virus might've cured everyone of the effects of the Gravity Bug, but there was no cure yet for the malice in men's hearts.

That wasn't her job anymore, though. Granted, she did enjoy some of her duties as second-in-command of the Guards. But not the seemingly endless meetings, all the redundant record keeping, and the constant adjusting of personnel schedules.

Marriage to Tony remained thrilling. And challenging. But she wanted more.

Just then a bright light flared in the sky, flashed across the black canvas of the night before she could even consider making a wish—though she certainly wasn't superstitious—and hit the horizon. Bursting into a magnificent dome of yellowish orange illumination. But the beautiful glow quickly began fading away. Reclaimed by the dark.

The meteorite—for that was what it had to have been—must've made a big bang, but she heard only silence. She glanced at Tony who was staring at the now empty space. "Think that landed on anyone?"

Her husband shook his head. "The odds would have been slim of it impacting in an inhabited area, even before." And these days there were a lot fewer people around out there.

They continued to stare in that direction for almost a full minute, but nothing happened and Kat's first queasy feeling at seeing the strike settled down to a faint foreboding. "Must've been really far away or we'd have heard something by now." She tried to remember about lightning—didn't every second before the thunder sounded mean it was another mile further away?

Tony nodded. "Probably so far we'll never hear anything. Nothing to worry about."

"If it was that distant, it must've been a massive explosion to look so huge here." And no way of saying what anyone there might be dealing with due to the impact. That thought led to another. "Perhaps it's time to take another trip outside." To search for more survivors they could invite into the FURC, and to take out more of the human predators preying on people out there. "We haven't even approached the outskirts of Orlando yet."

Her husband stiffened, but at least he refrained from sighing or shaking his head. "Trust me, those big urban areas...you don't want to see what's left." And likely he was right about that. Still.

"What about the suburbs? We could get closer, couldn't we?"

Now he shook his head. "The mobs would have spread across the entire metro area." And she knew Tony would know all about that, after Miami. Then they'd have turned on each other, the mob consuming itself rather than travel into the country because it hunted the easiest prey. He'd told her about that, too, and again he would know. She'd rather not see for herself. "As for searching those small towns and rural areas nearby again, would it do any good?"

Kat allowed herself a soft sigh. That first scouting trip, they'd taken out Henson and his cruel band of cutthroats, the biggest menace to survivors in the immediate vicinity of the FURC, convinced many of their neighbors to seek safety inside the compound, and—unknown to Kat, at least initially, released the Lift Virus into the wild. Subsequent excursions had yielded little in the way of finding more people they could bring back. Or more bad guys for her to fight. Consequently those trips had been a lot less exciting than she'd wished.

On the other hand, they had yet to venture very far afield. "We could go further from the compound while still staying away from the large urban areas." There had to be more survivors out there they could help. Somewhere.

"What brought this on?" Her husband sighed in her ear. "We can't save everyone." She knew that.

They'd done their best to persuade anyone they encountered—anyone decent and civilized anyway—to take shelter in the FURC. But many only wanted to hunker down in their homes. "With things fairly settled here though, we wouldn't be missed much if we took longer, searched some of the places we had decided were too distant before." And thanks to the Lift Virus, they were healthier and hardier than humans had ever been. "We can manage living rough longer too."

Tony took a step away from her and looked Kat in the eye. "But are you willing to be away from our home for so long? It might be months." He ran his hands up and down her arms. "And do you plan on dragging any survivors along with us as we go? Because sending them off on their own to make it back to the FURC wouldn't be safe, and would defeat the whole point."

She nodded reluctantly. "One of us would have to escort a group back." Whenever they discovered people who were worth inviting. And also willing to go.

"Which would add weeks, maybe months more to the mission. And keep us apart even more." Because they'd have to split up a lot of the trip anyway to cover the most ground. "It would be hell to go so long without you."

Kat smiled. Sometimes her husband could end up saying the most romantic things. "I know." She had already considered those difficulties in the past as she'd wondered about future scouting trips. "It's become so boring, though." She saw him frown. "I mean at work."

Now Tony looked like he wanted to laugh. "You love teaching those guys how to fight and shoot."

"Alright, I still enjoy *part* of my job." It was the only bit she found really fun, but he was right about that–she absolutely loved teaching the skills he and later Ken had taught her. "I've even turned our David into something of a badass."

"See, you're a miracle worker." Tony chuckled. "Where would the guards be without you whipping them into shape?"

She snorted. "Ken can do that just by growling. And glaring at them. It's not as if my skills are actually needed anymore." Not without a serious enemy to fight. "At least you've got an interesting problem to challenge you."

The officers in Security were more than capable of handling the day-to-day outbreaks of violence or other bad behavior without Tony's help. But he had been tasked with observing and evaluating all those new residents, in addition to certain older residents who had come under suspicion—and without any of them realizing they were being investigated. To unearth any moles the enemy might have slipped into the compound and prevent any more sabotage. But not all opponents of the FURC administration were actual enemies.

Her father had, eventually, publicly admitted the administration's role in creating the Lift Virus—he'd made it sound like a desperate attempt to deal with the Gravity Bug, which it basically *had* been, and as if all the unusual consequences had been unintended, which appeared to be true. However, he'd elided the fact that the entire federal government had been aware of the danger posed by the parasite for a long time. Years.

And he had glossed over the way he'd permitted citizens to be used as guinea pigs.

He had also waited to come out with the abbreviated truth until most everyone had already recovered from 'the cure'—Kat couldn't even think of the Lift Virus like that without scare quotes in her mind—and begun to see the benefits for themselves. Her father had not, however, been able to explain why it had been necessary to keep everything secret from almost everyone. Not in a way which satisfied anyone. And so, many people had grumbled about that for quite a while. Some continued to clash with the current leadership.

But life in the community continued to improve, and things had settled down and remained calm for a long time now.

Perhaps it was time to consider having a kid. It seemed as safe here as before the world started falling apart, maybe even safer. Pregnancy wouldn't be dull, though she certainly wasn't looking forward to it, and raising a child would be a challenge—one she wasn't sure she was up to. Just thinking about that made her queasy.

That swaying feeling in her stomach grew like a wave building within her, and alarm bells began going off in the back of her head. Then Tony grabbed her hand and they were running together across the roof as it began to buckle beneath them.

A roaring filled her head. Tony let go her hand, right before they reached the knee-high rim of concrete along the edge, and Kat dove over the parapet and off the roof.

Her training took over. Angling her body so she could deflect her momentum as she hit the ground and turn the impact into a roll. But the earth rushed up to meet her too soon.

Folding her head under her arms, she managed to relax into the premature collision—though it still felt like a giant's fist slamming into her. And rolled across the undulating ground—with poor form—as it settled back down. To where it belonged.

She slowed and came up into a crouch and conducted a swift mental inventory of her injuries—lots of bruising, but nothing felt broken or sprained. No sharp pains, so she should be good to go. Standing, she glanced around for Tony and realized it was *too* dark. "Power's out."

She heard a grunt in response and finally made out the blacker shadow of her husband as he rose to his feet a few yards away. And then brushed off his clothes, so he had to be alright.

Her hand automatically reaching for the FURCS pad she'd left up in their rooms, it hit her that communications would also be out as well as the lights. "I don't think that brought any buildings down, not as far as I can see." Around here, anyway.

Tony sighed loudly. "But until power's back on and we can see properly, we can't determine if these structures are still sound."

Kat nodded. "We'll have to assume they aren't. And until we have light and the FURCSnet working so people can call in, there'll be no way to assess the extent of damage across the compound."

"Thankfully there will be almost nobody in this section on a Friday night, but we'll have to clear the suites." Which were likely all occupied. Though so far no one had come running out.

"There may be injured." At least they were both extensively trained in first aid. "We can check faster if we split up."

Tony moved carefully across the broken ground to reach her. "Alright. I'll take the north half if you take the south. But go slow and be thorough. Don't want to miss anyone, much less injure ourselves."

She nodded. Thankfully he had refrained from suggesting they stay together—however much she'd have liked to—given he knew she could take care of herself. "And we'll need to grab our pads, for when power comes back." Hopefully that would be soon. "So I'll head for our rooms as soon as I've swept my half. Meet you there."

"Once we've done what we can for people here" —turning as he spoke, he started toward the closest door back into the building—"we probably ought to head for our respective offices." Which were on opposite ends of the compound. He entered the hotel, and at least there was the dim red glow of emergency lighting ahead of him.

Following her husband inside, she sighed. "Bob should already be coordinating Security's response, right?" The former sheriff, who was Tony's deputy, should be at their HQ. And no doubt Ken would've stayed late—with her off duty—and have everything under control at the Guard headquarters. That was where she wanted to be, regardless.

"As far as possible with no communications, I'm sure Kirkland's doing what he can. But I want to be there, as I'm sure you understand."

She nodded and started swiftly across the lobby toward Suite C as he headed the other way. Having talked with Sgt. Rose so she could do the paperwork to switch shifts around to give him the weekend off, Kat knew he would be here with his wife. And she'd overheard Ken making the reservations for them, so knew where to find the couple.

But even as she approached the door, it opened and Steve came running out, stuffing his shirt into his pants as he stumbled into the hall. Saw her and snapped a salute. "Lieutenant?"

"Is your wife alright?" The woman wasn't right behind him, and if she was injured it would explain his hurried exit and why he was alone.

"Colleen's fine. She's getting our things together." He shook his head. "But the bathroom's flooding. There's not much pressure though, so I'm sure there are more breaks. And without power the sensors can't shut the valves the way they're supposed to, so I have to manually turn off the supply into the building."

"Just make sure she gets out too. That you both stay outside, because it may not be safe inside."

Steve shook his head again but didn't argue. "I told her to take our stuff and head home. And after I've shut off the water, I'll head for HQ."

Kat sighed. "Negative, Sergeant. You'll see her home safe and make sure your boys and Red are alright." The Roses had adopted Kat's black Lab, and Red was part of their family now, but she still cared about the big lug. "By then the power should be restored and the net back up. You can call in then and see if we need you. And where."

Snapping another salute, he barked, "Yes, Lieutenant." And hustled past her.

She turned and followed him as far as the other hall, ran down that to the door to Suite A. Pounded on it, but got no immediate response. Continued to knock until the door swung open to reveal Alvin Fox of all people, standing there in a white silk shirt and crisp tan slacks. With his sleeves rolled up for work but looking relaxed and casual. "What?"

Kat tried not to grind her teeth. “Did you fail to notice the building shaking, Councilor?” Her mom, who headed the Community Council, called the man a thorn in her side. And described him as a terrible flirt. Thankfully he wasn’t trying to flirt with her, at the moment anyway. “I’m checking for injured and getting everyone out.”

“I’m fine.” She looked him over again, and this time noticed he was standing in his stockinged feet. “We’re both fine, and busy.” *We?*

Baring her teeth in a fake smile, she pushed the door open, forcing him to back up. “Nevertheless, I have to check. And you’ll—both of you, all of you?—need to evacuate the building.”

Fox glanced over his shoulder. She followed his gaze and saw Susan Wellman approaching from the sitting room. “Susan?” She wanted to ask what the woman was doing there, but it was awkward.

Kat considered the security officer—now a shift supervisor—a friend. Or had.

Susan shook her head. “It’s not what you think —this is a business meeting.” Her smart casual outfit supported that assertion. And there was nothing intimate in the atmosphere, despite the location.

Well, the woman had been a business major before the lockdown, had returned to those studies as soon as classes had started up again. And Alvin Fox did represent the commercial concerns within their community. But these luxury suites seemed an odd place to meet, even if they desired privacy. And Fox had a reputation.

Kat should probably be worried about Susan's—under the circumstances—but now was not the time for that. "Doesn't matter what I think, I'm just glad to see you're uninjured." She frowned at Fox. "You too, Councilor." Though mainly because tending to *anyone* who was wounded would only delay dealing with all the other problems she would undoubtedly run into.

Susan nodded briskly. "Loose objects got tossed around. The lights going out was frustrating—more so the net being down." She waggled her pad in one hand. "But no big deal. Here, anyway. They'll need me at Security, I suppose."

Kat shrugged. "Probably, but it's hard to say at the moment where help might be most needed. Except for this—someone should escort Councilor Fox home. He's too important to let him go back on his own. And since Chief Nelson and I have to clear the rest of the building, I suggest you see to that."

Susan simply nodded again. "I'll get him home safe, then head to headquarters. Maybe I'll beat the boss back to the office."

"Don't try. Things may be difficult out there, so take it slow and careful. You won't be any use if you get hurt by your own carelessness." She let an edge into her tone with that last comment and hoped the woman understood the double meaning to the caution.

Without waiting for a response, which probably would've been merely a nod anyway, she turned and hurried out the door, down the hall, and toward the stairs. She'd clear the two sets of rooms above, then hopefully meet Tony for a quick kiss before they had to go their separate ways again, and retrieve her pad for whenever it would work. Then begin a long trek across the compound. *Wonder what other surprises I may find along the way.*

Thankfully, however much the shaking had rattled them, the damage didn't appear to be that bad.

Chapter 2

When You Miss a Falling Star

9:40 p.m. Friday, May 27th
First floor of the FURC Medical Center

DAVID CAREFULLY LIFTED two thick tomes from Amita's desk with one hand and placed the tray in the cleared space with the other. "Make sure you drink the coffee before it cools off." He had added a plate of cheese cubes and power potato chips in case she got peckish. And actually thought to eat.

Glancing up from whatever she'd been doing on her workpad, Amita gave a smile of thanks and took a sip from the mug before bending her head back to the screen. She'd been a woman obsessed for three years now, and David felt somewhat responsible for that. The least he could do was bring her some food now and then so she didn't starve.

"I'm sure that must be fascinating"—he nodded at her pad—"but remember your brain needs fuel as well as your body. Anyway, I assume that's still the case."

Amita sighed and tapped the screen to mark her place, then picked up a piece of cheese. "Yes, we still require food, though our bodies are absorbing those nutrients more efficiently. What's really fascinating though—and that's a weak word for it—are the most recent results from your latest bloodwork."

Groaning, David wished he'd brought coffee for himself. Bad enough being a guinea pig, even worse to have to hear all about it without something to take the edge off. "What now?" He'd better sit down for this.

She knew how he felt but widened her grin. "It seems your system has started to manufacture vitamin C."

He scratched his forehead. "That's a good thing then, right?" So far all the physical changes caused by his altered DNA had been improvements. But as much medical knowledge as he'd picked up through these conversations, there was a whole heck of a lot more he didn't know. And much of what she'd tried to tell him he still didn't understand.

Taking another sip, she leaned back in her chair and shook her head. At his ignorance, he was sure, not in answer to his question. "Humans, unlike the rest of the animal world, can't create C in their own bodies. Or rather, we seem to have lost that ability, somewhere in the distant past. It's essential to good health, but we have to consume it. Or we did. Now we appear to have regained the capability, thanks to the Lift Virus. Or maybe it's just you."

David nodded his understanding. Presumably, then, he wouldn't have to keep taking it as a supplement. He also knew that while many of the changes he'd been experiencing were also happening to anyone who'd had 'the flu'—such as his vastly improved immune response—some hadn't appeared in others yet. On the other hand, some people who were part of the first wave of flu 'victims' had experienced improvements he hadn't.

Like the way Lt. Miles could now see in the dark as well as or better than a cat. While he still seemed blind as a bat at night. "Well, I've no doubt you will figure it all out sooner or later." Amita was brilliant and one of the best epidemiologists around. Which was why they'd chosen her to lead the research into the effects of the Lift Virus. "But eat first, work can wait."

She sighed dramatically but seemed pleased by his concern. "Alright." She popped the cheese cube she'd picked up earlier into her mouth and grabbed a handful of chips. "But what about you?" She lifted an eyebrow. "Don't you need to eat too?"

"I already had supper. But then I got called out to escort a couple of newcomers here to get their 'flu shots'. As soon as I handed them over to the nurse, I headed to the cafeteria to get you something, since I knew you wouldn't have thought to get anything for yourself."

Amita swallowed and nodded. "Well, then. After you've gotten the asylum seekers settled in their new quarters, how about you come back and escort me home? And we can see to our other needs."

David blushed. They'd been seeing each other a long time now, but he remained determined to take things slow. She seemed determined to break down his resolve. Still, at the end of the long day it wasn't like either of them would have energy for more than a bit of a cuddle. "Alright. Maybe there'll be something new worth watching on the viewing pad."

She shook her head in mock exasperation, with him? Perhaps it was in denial of the possibility that the Media Centre might've made something decent. Recently, anyway. Ever since Caroline Sanderson—the famed actress who had been running the place—had been elected First Councilor, students had been left in charge of producing 'entertainment' for viewing on the FURCSnet. And the quality of the shows had rapidly deteriorated.

Washing down a mouthful of chips with a third sip of her coffee, Amita waved him off. "We'll worry about what to do at home later. For now, let me get back to work. So I can finish it before you return to give me more grief."

He started to stand—and almost fell as the room shook side to side with sudden violence, heaving up and thudding back down at the same time.

Clutching the edge of the desk with one hand to steady himself, he reached out with the other when he saw the huge glass jar that had sat on top of a filing cabinet sailing through the air. Somehow managed to catch it against the flat of his palm and slam it down onto the desktop without breaking it. Then sighed as the tremor subsided.

Amita's chair had been thrown forward against the desk, pinning her against it. The food had flown off the tray, and her cup of coffee had slid all the way across to crash on the floor. And she herself leaned forward, staring glassy-eyed at the preserved brain, which still swayed in its solution inside the jar right in front of her face.

David blew out the breath he hadn't realized he was holding and laughed nervously. "That thing almost brained you."

Her eyes snapped into focus, and she pushed off the desk, shoving the chair back and glaring at him. "I've only kept it around in case you needed a transplant." The quip only made him laugh harder, hysterically. Which made her purse her lips.

Then he noticed the lights overhead had grown dim. "Emergency backup power?" That would be a remnant from the days when the compound had relied on the regional grid. And hadn't been required in three and a half years. Not since the attacks on the FURCSnet, which he checked on his pad and found to be down.

Coming around the desk, Amita shoved him toward the door. "And there are likely people who *did* get injured out there. Every able hand will be needed to help."

"Yes, Dr. Harker." David snatched her rumpled lab coat off the hook on the back of the door, tossed it to her, and swung the door open. "Go get...er...fix 'em."

She grabbed his shirt as she strode past, pulling him along behind her as she stepped into the corridor. "You can help as well."

"I should head to HQ, see whether—" He cut off the protest as he saw the mess in the hall. He would have to clear a path for her to the clinic section. He darted ahead, bent down to sweep up an armload of bandages, shoved them into the box they had spilled out of, and set that on top of a gurney he had to pick up off the floor too.

Pushing that against the wall, he moved on and removed the next obstacle and the next. Wondered why such clutter would've been permitted along the corridors of the medical center. He wondered even more about the quake. In Florida? Had it been the New Madrid fault in Missouri or wherever? Hard to believe they'd feel it so strongly here.

He glanced back often, to make sure Amita was still with him, and always saw her tidying up behind him. By the time they'd turned down a couple more short hallways, they'd been joined by a sullen nurse and a somewhat dazed-looking orderly. And David was optimistic he wouldn't be needed here, that she would send him to join the rest of the guards. Then their little convoy reached the main ward.

The nurse practitioner on duty was examining a patient on a bed sporting a nasty-looking laceration across his forehead while a sister was trying to help another back into his bed, who must've fallen to the floor. The orderly they'd brought with them rushed to help her.

Just those two patients, but the clinic didn't get much business these days. And so staffing was kept short. Enough for the usual run of accidents, but it wouldn't suffice for a sudden influx of injured. And David expected exactly that.

The second sister scooted past Amita and started cleansing the cut that one patient had somehow gotten, and the nurse practitioner turned to peer at Amita with a grim expression. "The two med techs, who are on duty and should be around somewhere, have yet to appear. I'll assume they're injured. And the pair of newcomers your young friend brought in are in the exam room. I haven't had an opportunity to check on them, so I'm glad you're here, Doctor."

Amita nodded briskly. "It looks as if you've got everything under control here. But it could get hectic soon. Hopefully all the off-duty personnel are on their way. Until then, you've got me and David here to help."

He nodded and, thinking about the couple he'd brought and his responsibility for their welfare, ran out of the ward and into the large exam room to one side of the lobby. He didn't notice Amita following, not until he braked hard at seeing the shambles the place was in. And the middle-aged man and woman lying tangled together in a heap on the floor covered with debris.

Chunks of the ceiling, thankfully only some thin pieces of plaster, had fallen on them. As well as two small steel stools on which they'd probably been sitting. Not enough to pin them down. But David immediately hauled them off, set them out of the way. Then the man moaned and proved that he, at least, still lived.

Amita bent down to take the woman's pulse and flip up one of her eyelids. "Unconscious and probably in shock." She switched to examine the man. "I think he's got a concussion, and it looks like he may have a contusion on the back of his head, but I can't be sure without moving him, and I don't want to do that until he's properly immobilized. Let's hope he isn't bleeding internally."

David grimaced. "And they just got their shots, so neither of them will be experiencing the benefits yet." Only the flu-like side effects appeared swiftly. "What do you need me to do?"

"Bring over one of the gurneys, help me get the woman off him gently and lift her onto it. We'll get her onto one of the beds and tuck her underneath a blanket to keep her warm." As he hurried over and grabbed the closest gurney, she continued. "Then I want you to run back to the ward and ask the nurse practitioner to come quick. You can't help with this man."

After they'd lifted the woman, and as they were rolling her over to a bed, Amita shook her head. "I don't want you to forget—however fast you can heal now, a traumatic injury or bleeding out can still kill you before those 'benefits' kick in. So remember to be careful, David."

"That goes for you too, Doc."

As he started racing back to the ward, she called out behind him. "Once you've sent someone to help me, search the rest of the building and see if you can find those two missing med techs. Or anybody else here who might be injured."

He found the nurse practitioner already leaving the ward, heading toward the exam room, assuming Amita needed her help. He briefly told her the situation there, and she gestured to one of the sisters to follow her.

Charging across the room and into the opposite corridor from how he'd originally come, he reached the ambulance bay, where the med techs often hung out. So they could head out swiftly if they got a call —or so they said. David thought they just liked being away from the activity in the clinic.

When he got there, he discovered that two huge and heavy horizontal filing cabinets had been flung across the hall and were blocking the wide swinging doors so they wouldn't open. He gazed through one of the tiny, blurry, plastic windows in the doors and saw the two med techs. Sitting slumped against the side of one of the ambulances.

"Guys, what's keeping you from *driving* out?"

They both looked up as he shouted, then one of them hollered back. "That quake or whatever it was buckled the bay doors. They won't open." And that meant the ambulance couldn't get out to pick up the injured. Thankfully there were plenty of the electric carts out there—hopefully undamaged—which could be pressed into service. But it wasn't the same.

"Alright. Let me see if I can shift these cabinets so you can get out this way." Then at least they'd be able to help Amita and the others in the clinic. And he could head over to HQ.

David hugged one of the bulky metal monsters, shoved his shoulder against the surface that leaned down toward the ground, and pushed with his legs. But it didn't budge. What he needed was some sort of lever.

Racing back down the hall a bit, he found a pole for IV bags he'd passed along the way and carried it back and wedged the edge of the base into a tiny gap between the cabinet and the wall. He put his shoulder once more against the angled metal surface, but this time he pried with the pole as he pushed. For a long moment nothing happened.

Then the metal groaned in protest and suddenly the cabinet fell over onto its feet with a great clunk. David tried to keep shoving, to get it completely out of the way of the door, but again it refused to budge an inch.

If he'd been smart, he would have placed something that slid under the other end before he righted it, but it was too late now. However, there would be less friction with the floor the lower he could get for pushing. After heaving a huge sigh to shuffle off his frustration with himself, he squatted down and put his shoulder as low against the side of the cabinet as he could and still get good leverage. Then he began pushing with his legs and driving his shoulder at as close to horizontal an angle as possible, felt the cabinet shift slightly, and kept shoving. And slowly the thing moved, bit by bit.

Eventually he got it completely clear of the door it had been blocking, then pulled it open and called to the med techs. No use bothering to try to clear that other door, even with their help, as no one would be bringing any patients through this way, not anytime soon.

The two men nodded their thanks and sprinted down the corridor toward the clinic. David thought about following, to check on Amita. But it had only been a few minutes since he left her, and with those two med techs and whoever else would show up, he certainly wouldn't be needed. Would only get in the way if he tried to help there.

He went back to the elevator—not that he would try to use it after the quake, but he wanted to check that no one else had and been trapped or something—and found it sitting open and empty. Sprinting up the stairs to the second floor, he took a few minutes to look around Dr. Cummings' office and lab. Even the mad scientist wasn't likely to be working late on a Friday night, though. And no one was there.

The few private rooms up here and two overflow wards were all empty too—none having been in use for a very long time, David wasn't surprised. Ducking into one of the bathrooms, he splashed cold water on his face. And thanked God the clinic still had running water. With the backup power on, the sensors would've shut the valves to cut the flow if pipes had burst, but apparently they hadn't. At least, not here.

He ran his wet hands through his hair, then returned to the stairs and skipped down to the ground floor, turned left and continued down the long hallway until he reached one of the emergency exits.

Stepping outside and into an almost pitch-black dark, David took a while to get his bearings. His old friend Ken was a good boss, but he did *not* tolerate excuses, and as it was Chief Cameron would want to know what had taken David so long.

Thankfully the Guard HQ wasn't that far. Picking his way carefully across the grass in the black of a night unilluminated but for a gibbous moon and a smattering of faint stars overhead, he headed south until he reached the concrete walkway which would take him to the main thoroughfare. And from there it was a straight shot to—

His train of thought cut off as he heard puffing, then saw a monster emerging from the shadows up ahead, shuffling toward him. Then his eyes focused and he could see it was actually two people, one trying rather unsuccessfully to carry the other who appeared to be injured.

David ran forward. "What happened?"

The short, burly fellow who had the injured guy draped across his back answered breathlessly. “The idiot was in such a rush to get out of the building he jumped out a second-story window. One of the tech dorms. You know what those geeks are like.”

David nodded and grinned. “And what are you then? Construction worker?”

The broad-shouldered man inhaled deeply before shaking his head. “Nope, I’m a tech geek too. But I guess I’ve got more sense than some. It looked like he landed on his feet alright, but based on how he’d screamed before passing out I’m guessing he broke a leg or something.”

“Come on, then.” David came around one side, slid an arm under the unconscious man’s shoulder, and motioned his friend to take the other side. “We don’t want his legs swinging more than we can help under the circumstances.” If only they could call an ambulance. “Grab my other hand under his knees.” He slid his arm under the injured man’s legs. “And we’ve made a chair to carry him to the clinic.” They wouldn’t be able to move fast like that, but it wasn’t far. And once they had gotten this guy into the good hands of the sisters, he’d head back out again.

Chapter 3

Makes No Difference

9:40 p.m. Friday, May 27th
FURC Detention Center, Women's Ward

SARA LAY FLAT on the cot in her cell, staring at the ceiling as she tried to ignore the rustling sounds made by the other inmates. And thought about her life as she did every night. One of the few long-term prisoners, this place had become her world, and she was the only one here who had worked for Security. That made things difficult.

But then, she knew she didn't deserve easy, and she certainly couldn't contemplate release, not after what she'd done. Holding her gun to the head of the newly elected First Councilor in aid of an attempted overthrow of the administration would never be forgiven by anyone in authority. Especially since she'd been an officer tasked with protecting the community. How could they ever let her out to roam free?

Not inside the compound, anyway, and she was glad they hadn't decided to expel her. Even though she was now free of the Gravity Bug and immune to its effects, which included a horrible death, making her way alone on the outside would be a frightening and miserable experience. Even with the improved health the Lift Virus had given her and all her training, she would have to scavenge to survive. And always be on guard against the predators, human and animal, out there. Seeking the weak. No, compared to that, life in the detention center was quite cozy.

Three square meals a day was nothing to sneeze at, and if this mattress was a little thin, she still had a roof over her head and a pillow to rest it on. Most of the prisoners here only stayed a few days or a few weeks at worst, waiting while their cases were adjudicated and punishments decided upon—and those almost never included continued incarceration.

Only those found to be an ongoing threat to the safety of the community, like Sara, were kept locked away. And she couldn't blame them for that. Didn't now, anyway.

At first she'd railed against all of them—Kat and Caroline and Paul and anyone she could think of to blame. Against fate. Against Alice Kittner, the dean who had recruited her into the coup. And who Sara had, however inadvertently, shot in the head, killed as the woman was ranting about revolution and trying to stir one up. Kittner had never stood a chance of success, and Sara had been foolish to follow her—but it had taken a long time to admit that to herself. To admit all her bad choices.

Her rage had mostly spent itself by the time the force of the Lift Virus had hit. And three days later, when she'd started to recover, she no longer had the strength to maintain her anger. So Sara had shifted to self-pity.

Still playing the blame game, she had spent her days feeling sorry for herself, even as she'd accepted more and more of the guilt for her own actions. She had become depressed, and seriously contemplated suicide. After all, what did she have to look forward to besides mere survival?

Maybe it would've been better if they'd expelled her from the FURC. However horrible, and short, a life that might've been, there would have been some slim chance of finding...redemption.

Then again, without all these long, quiet, boring nights forcing her into self-examination, would she have come to the point of wanting that?

Sighing, Sara thought about her former friends and the lives they were leading today. The turnover in detainees meant a constant source of news about goings on in the community, and things were going well for most. Challenges remained, keeping things interesting—for those who were out and about, free to meet them—but the existential crises threatening the compound had been dealt with. Life was good.

For those she had wronged, and even for her, as constrained as her current existence was. For Paul, Kat, and the rest of her former colleagues, life probably kept getting better. But as for Sara, she saw no hope for improvement in her own—

The world around her lurched and roared. Her cot threw her to the ground and she rolled under it, mind grasping for understanding. But even as that came—an explanation for the earth shaking seemed obvious a moment later—the heaving began to subside. Alarms—no, it was her ears that rang.

Crawling out from under her cot, Sara saw that her cell door had opened and the dim red emergency lights turned on, which meant the power was off. All the doors should be unlocked, then. The contingency was for prisoners needing to evacuate in case of a fire, in the event officers on duty were unable to unlock everything in time. Or at all. In case of disaster.

Sara couldn't smell smoke, and since the sprinklers were not spraying foam she figured no fire had started. This being Florida, they'd never had earthquake drills, but she had a vague notion they should do the same as for a fire—get out.

An open cell, unlocked doors, and the excuse to go outside. A tantalizing taste of freedom awaiting, already bitter for the knowledge that it couldn't last long. One way or another she'd be back in this cell. Better then to wait for the officers to escort her out, if they came.

As the ringing in her ears diminished though, it was replaced by an increasing volume of incoherent voices, the other women shouting questions, yelling as they discovered their own open doors. And Sara couldn't let them corner her in a cell.

Rolling across the small space and onto her feet near the bars, she slipped out into the wide featureless corridor barely ahead of a couple other inmates escaping their own little prisons and looking around in confusion.

The short older woman with black hair hanging over one shoulder in a single thick braid boasted of a terrible temper. Arguments with her easily escalated into fights that saw her cooling her heels in here. Back before she had become an inmate herself, Sara had often been the one to arrest Becky, so she knew the woman wasn't a serious threat.

But beyond her, further down the hall, a broad-shouldered blonde a head taller than Sara glared at her through the heavy shadows. Another long-term resident, the inappropriately named Marigold was a mixed martial artist who'd been put in here because she had beaten her boyfriend to a bloody pulp. And she'd repeatedly said she planned to do the same to Sara when she got the chance. Which it looked like fate had now given her.

The other 'residents' came cautiously out of the cells, and Sara thought furiously. None of the other women liked her. It would only take the suggestion for them to gang up and overwhelm her. Thanks to the training Kat and Tony had given her, she might be able to handle just Marigold. But she was under no illusion she could take on all of them at the same time.

And she couldn't count on being rescued by the officers on duty, who hadn't shown up yet. Neither Michelle nor Greg. And no telling when—or if—they would, under the circumstances.

Sara called out, "All the doors to the outside will have automatically unlocked. So we can evacuate in an emergency. But as soon as the power comes on, everything will lock down again."

There was a general stir, then a woman down at the far end of the corridor must've tried the door to the sally port. "She's right. We can get out. And I'm not waiting."

That prisoner flung the door wide and went out the one on the other side, continued on through the intake room and presumably across the lobby. Out of the building, to freedom. And her escape sparked a mass exodus, leaving only Marigold and Becky behind. Probably the only ones who'd had the time to think about Sara. And what they might want to do to her.

But Becky glanced back and forth and, after the briefest of hesitations, darted past the big blonde in a mad dash for the exit. Marigold, though, only had eyes for Sara.

Taking up a classic kickboxing stance, as if preparing for a formal bout—though Marigold wasn't a person who respected the rules—the woman smiled in anticipation.

Sara, however, hadn't trained to fight for sport. While Kat and Tony had both pressed her not to use more force than necessary, every officer understood their life was potentially on the line in any confrontation. She had been taught to end every altercation as quickly as possible.

Going to one knee, she put a look of pleading on her face. "Please, just go. Get out while—"

As fast as Marigold's shin sailed through where Sara's head had been, it was no longer there. Since she'd rolled forward at the same time. She slammed her heel into the side of the knee supporting the other woman's weight, causing Marigold to crumple to the ground. A brief cry of pain had suddenly cut off as her head hit the concrete floor. Hard. Knocking herself out cold.

Of course she might regain consciousness soon and be able to make it outside on her own, but Sara should properly drag the woman out of the building right away. Before she came round.

Only, that would leave Sara even more vulnerable to the others as she exited, and some might have decided to wait and ambush her when she left. And it wasn't as if there was any imminent danger facing anyone who remained inside.

The layout of the square, single-story detention center flashed into her head. She could follow those other women through the sally port and intake room to the lobby and the front door. Into the Yard. She didn't fancy mingling out there with the other prisoners, but the ten-foot-high fence—lacking razor or barbed wire on top—would be easy enough to scale. Or she could go the opposite direction.

The door on the other end opened on a hall she could take to the kitchen or break room at the back, where the officers on duty spent most of their time, or to three more corridors running back toward the front of the building. Two of those stretched along a string of rooms, facilities for the inmates. Study areas. Work centers for the jobs they could do to earn credits while they were here, a small gym, showers, and other utilities. One set of each for the men and the women, and no connecting doors between. And both those passageways dead-ended.

But that last hall, on the other side of the building, was just like the one she was standing in. With seven cells down each side, and all fourteen usually occupied by male prisoners, and some of them were real hard cases. Those men posed a serious danger to everyone, and it might be imminent.

Sara didn't know how long it would take for one of them to discover all the doors had been unlocked —it wasn't something shared with the inmates—but they might have already. And no telling what they'd do when they did.

Even so, Sara had a more immediate concern—there was still no sign of Michelle or Greg. And she was worried about them. Despite everything and in spite of the circumstances, she continued to consider them colleagues. Though she and Michelle Mori had never gotten along. And Greg Belaford had not even joined Security before she'd been incarcerated here.

But either or both could've been injured in that quake. Be lying injured in the break room or somewhere else with no one coming to their aid. Or they might well have raced to the men's ward and gotten stuck in the middle of a melee. Or maybe they were even now outside, at the front of the building trying to shepherd the inmates who'd evacuated.

But those two would be hard-pressed to handle a couple dozen or so freed prisoners by themselves, so she needed to help, even if they failed to welcome her assistance.

Hastening to the door at her end of the hall, she crouched. Took a deep breath. Flung it open wide, then dived into the similarly dim passage and rolled across the broad space to the far side—scanning her surroundings as they whirled around and seeing no one. Came up into another crouch against the wall, then glanced back and forth to confirm the corridor was empty except for herself.

Sara was trying to decide which way to go when she heard the scream.

Chapter 4
Who You Are

9:40 p.m. Friday, May 27th
FURC Director's Office, Administration Building

JONATHAN MILES SAT behind his broad desk and sighed with relief as he read once again the encrypted communication they'd received a little over an hour ago. From the Omega Squad, a special team he'd help put together, recruited from various intelligence agencies. The report that they had rendered useless the last remaining nuclear weapons outside the US had taken another load off his shoulders and allowed him to finally send the message that would begin the decommissioning of America's arsenal.

Civilization might be collapsing, but at least the threat of some madman taking advantage of that to annihilate their enemies should be over. Too much destruction had already been unleashed around the world. But every effort had been made to eliminate all the stockpiles of weapons of mass destruction, including chemical and biological. Hopefully humanity—what was left of it—was now safe. At least from those particular perils.

Rebuilding could become the focus, though the task loomed mountainous ahead of them, especially since he hadn't been able to complete setting up the FURC system. Final approval to begin construction of the Northeast complex hadn't come when he had been forced to seal this compound. The Midwestern facility remained unfinished and almost completely unstaffed. And those FURCs would have provided a lot of help.

Grateful the satellite they used to communicate with still operated, he regretted so few people could actually use it. Thankfully he'd received regular reports from the crew constructing that special FURC facility in the desert Southwest, but Tekihara at the compound in the Northwest had never even replied to his first message. Sent three and a half years ago.

Verity had warned him about Tekihara, but she hadn't been able to be specific, and he had not been able to prevent the woman's appointment anyway—his amanuensis had also failed to warn him of Governor Roberts' plans, the actions that had forced the closing of the compound earlier than optimal. Verity claimed not to have known—and that might even be true, since her knowledge of the future was obviously incomplete. Still, he felt sure she was holding back *something.* Even though he could not imagine why she would, under the circumstances.

He looked up at the closed door to his office and wondered if she was still out there in her own—he'd a vague impression of insisting she go home, but he knew she wouldn't necessarily have listened.

Actually, Verity only worked late anymore when they had confidential reports to review. Those were all kept in encrypted files on the FURCSnet. Everything cleared for sharing with the Council went onto paper and into unsightly binders—Miles shoved his inside the drawers of the handsome cherrywood filing cabinets lining the left wall of his office.

Admiring them for a moment, he then frowned at the crystal 'Flame of Freedom' award sitting atop one. They'd given him that for his work holding the federal government accountable to its citizens, back when he was an idealistic young lawyer. These days he had some sympathy with his old CIA pals. Some things should be kept secret.

And anything shared with the Council might as well be announced to the public, so he withheld the information he believed needed to be kept close—of course Verity had access to it all, and Miles confided everything to his wife Caroline. And they did share most secrets with Tony and Ken, eventually, as both men needed to know. But disseminating that information even to such a small extent made it difficult to maintain operational security.

But they didn't keep so many secrets that it was necessary to work this late most nights. Still, it had become habit with Miles back when he and Caroline wanted people to assume they were at odds, and he couldn't seem to break it. Not that it mattered any. Since she had been elected First Councilor, his wife now worked as late as he ever had. So why go home to an empty house?

That was why he often stayed long after the rest of his staff had left the building, even Verity, though a bit of a push was usually required to make her go. Leaving him here alone. The only one remaining on this floor, anyway, unless she was still here...

And his mind was wandering again.

Taking off his glasses, then pinching the bridge of his nose to ease the headache he couldn't seem to shake, he turned his attention back to his workpad. Opening the encrypted file containing the latest signal intelligence Verity had compiled for him, he began reading. What little there was.

While the FURC communications array continued to monitor transmissions carried over the various cellular networks, there was little to hear. Most of the infrastructure had degraded past the point of usefulness. And most of the country was now without power, so people couldn't recharge their phones even if it would've done them any good.

Technicians had constructed several short-wave radios in the FURC labs though, and ham operators around the world were reporting on their local conditions. Such transmissions were recorded and the information collated, by Verity or one of her trusted team, and that provided the bulk of their knowledge of what was happening out there.

The survivors wisely refrained from giving their specific locations. And they had stopped asking for assistance they must've realized would never come. But humans had to share, and all the stories of pain and hardship, struggle and survival, triumph in adversity—they painted a vivid picture of what people were going through across the country. Miles would have preferred not to see.

But he made himself read through every report to maintain his motivation, even as he regretted not being able to do more for them. Yet.

The FURC had welcomed thousands of refugees from the surrounding area into the compound, into their community. But they no longer had the room or resources to absorb many more. Though it hardly seemed likely that many remained in the vicinity, and they couldn't, practically speaking, send search parties farther out than they already had.

Releasing the Lift Virus into the wild would be a boon to many, eventually. Those who lived through the initial impact. And the people who died from it wouldn't likely have survived anyway, would probably have suffered a much worse fate from the hands of the human predators pillaging the countryside or those violent madmen who'd been compromised by the Gravity Bug, or have fallen to that very infection themselves. All horrible ways to go.

Still he felt awful about doing what he'd known he had to do—everything he could to ensure that the Lift Virus spread as far and as fast as possible. And now he could only guess how successful that operation had been.

Soon they'd have to start spreading out. Find a few towns that had weathered the collapse well and build them up, use those to launch expeditions further afield to search for more communities to add to the network. The plan had been for the other FURC directors to do the same until they could unite those separate sets of sanctuaries into one vast array with all the resources his community currently enjoyed.

So much for his plans. He still hoped to salvage the original concept, though the challenge would be much greater without the efforts of the other FURC communities. At least he should be able to draw on the resources at the Southwest facility. And assuming the situation at the Northwest FURC—whatever the difficulty there was—could be fixed, they should eventually be able to contribute. It would all take a lot longer than—

Suddenly he was thrown half up out of his chair as the building buckled beneath him. His first idea, to duck underneath his desk, he quickly abandoned as he remembered Verity might still be in the outer office. As everything was shaking he half-stumbled around the desk.

He had just rounded the corner when one of the heavy filing cabinets came crashing down into him, smashing into his thigh and sending him to the carpet. A sharp pain seared across his forehead. Wiping a weary hand across his brow, it came back covered in blood. Of course, head wounds bled a lot.

Lying on his side and pinned down by the huge cabinet, he gazed across the carpet and noticed that bloody award close at hand, realized it must've been what cut him. How ironic—the award itself and now how it had wounded him.

Then the blood began to run down into one eye and he knew he needed to get up and clean himself. The building no longer shook, though he thought he could still feel a slight sway, so he should get up and see to his own wounds and start searching for other victims. Of an earthquake?

No time to think about that at the moment. He tried to shift his leg out from under the fallen furniture, but the first feeble movement brought intense pain and a scream to his throat, and convinced him to stop. He stared at the closed oak door, wondered if there had been anyone near enough to have heard his shout. He called out—"In here! Need..."—could feel his voice weaken—"help..."—then trail off at the end.

Hopefully someone had heard *that*, since he did not think he could manage more. He knew that his leg was likely broken—at least a partial fracture from the blow—and he needed to get that treated. Soon.

He tried to lift the filing cabinet enough so that he could shove it off his legs but found there wasn't enough strength in his arms, and no leverage. Pulling himself over to the door wasn't an option, then. Much less crawling across the floor to the elevator—the stairs rather, as he belatedly noticed the dim red emergency lighting and realized the power was out. Only things with batteries would be running. Until those ran down.

Once someone fixed whatever had gone wrong, however, help should come. Though thinking of all the possible problems with the experimental power system scared him. Far more than his own perilous predicament.

Shoving those concerns aside—it wasn't as if he could do anything about them anyway—and placing his hands against the corners of the top of the filing cabinet, he put all his—failing—energy into another attempt to shift the thing off his legs. To no avail.

He'd just have to wait for someone to find him. The building wouldn't be completely empty. If anyone remained uninjured inside, they'd hopefully be searching for anyone who needed help. Like him.

His mind felt fuzzy, and Miles worried he'd lost too much blood to think straight. Worried he could be bleeding internally, might require medical intervention more urgently than he'd thought. He could be dying.

He took a deep breath to help him calm down—panicking never did any good—and reminded himself that his body would be healing faster and better thanks to the changes brought by the Lift Virus. He would last as long as he needed to. And there was a lot he still had to do.

David showed promise, especially now that he'd gotten back to his studies—the boy would become a good lawyer one day, and the community could use the guidance he'd be able to give. And Miles wanted to continue mentoring him the same way he'd been mentored by Hollingsworth.

He also had ideas for the future, potential plans he hadn't written down, much less shared with anyone. And since things had become a lot less rushed here, he had been meaning to spend more time with his daughter Kat but somehow hadn't gotten around to making the time. Of course, she had her own life now, busy between her job and marriage.

And probably little room to squeeze in a couple hours with her father, but at least he never worried. Not about Kat, who was so capable. Who had Tony to watch out for her and God watching over her, to a miraculous degree as Miles himself had seen.

But he did worry about Caroline. Always a little reckless and unaware of it, of pushing too hard. He needed to check on her, make sure she was alright.

Sighing, he reached into his pants pocket to get his personal pad before realizing that the net would be down with the power. Maybe Verity was still out there, on her way to check on him. Of course. Even if she had already left Admin, she knew he'd stayed behind and would return. He could always count on Verity.

Chapter 5

Playing with Fire

9:45 p.m. Friday, May 27th
Leaving the Administration Building

VERITY PUSHED THROUGH a side door and left the building with a brisk stride, then forced herself to slow down. As much as she'd enjoy shedding her shoes and jacket and sitting on the sofa at home with a nice glass of wine, she needed to get her head out of work to be able to relax. And the first step in doing that would be ambling along and enjoying the walk rather than rushing.

One benefit of working late as she had tonight—the elderly couple living in her house would already have settled into their rooms. With David gone, and after the unfortunate incident with her housekeeper Crystal, Verity had found the then newcomers from

Charlesberg to stay and take care of the now too-big-for-her place.

She liked having someone else there. And liked even more that they were quiet, kept to themselves, and largely left her alone. Better if it were Anya and Tate, but last she knew they were living on Florida's forgotten coast—too far away to even have any idea how they were coping. Worrying about them would do no good when she could do nothing, particularly when she needed to destress.

So, slip off her shoes in the foyer. Then pad into the kitchen and pour herself half a glass of that nice Pinot Grigio she'd opened—their wine stockpile had gotten low and the price per bottle had skyrocketed accordingly. Turn on a little light jazz to play in the background as she snuggled—

Suddenly she hit the cement walkway, scraping her hands and banging a knee, felt the ground sway violently under her. She curled into a ball, wrapped her arms around her head, and prayed—and kept on praying until the earth stopped shaking.

Once it had, Verity carefully uncurled. Placed a hand where the concrete had split and winced, tried to get her bearings.

David. She'd dropped her purse in the upheaval and scrabbled around in the dark to find where it had fallen. Pulling out her FURCS pad and turning that on provided some much-needed illumination—

but it wouldn't connect. So it wasn't only the lights here that had gone out.

With no idea where her son might be, she would not be able to check to see he was alright until communications were restored, and before she could do that she'd have to get the power back.

Miles. At least she knew where Jon would be, in his office. Coming out from under his desk, at least if he'd noticed the earthquake in the first place. She wouldn't be surprised to find he'd been so absorbed in reading reports that he'd missed the entire event completely. Either way he'd probably be frustrated by the mess it would've made.

Struggling to her feet and shoving her right foot into the shoe that had fallen off, Verity used her pad as a flashlight and began stumbling her way back to the administration building. She'd need to check on Jon. But before that she'd have to see what could be done to return power to the compound.

The clinic had a generator for emergencies, but not enough gas to keep it running very long. And it would be next to impossible to assess damage, help the injured, or do much of anything until they could communicate to coordinate the response. Even the electric carts they relied on for getting around—and those would be especially useful right now—needed the main power source up and running, because the batteries under their hoods wouldn't last long. The engines relied on a continual current from the wireless nodes. There were the ambulances, and plenty of private vehicles which were hybrid, but still.

She wouldn't even know if the communications array on the Admin roof was working until they had power on again. Hopefully the FURCSnet remained operational, or rather would be once it rebooted.

The looming dark hulk of the building ahead of her didn't appear to be damaged on the outside—as far as she could see in the nearly pitch-black night—but inside had to be a different story. Power hadn't failed for no reason.

And she refused to speculate on what that could be, she'd see for herself soon enough. Set in motion whatever needed to be done to fix things. Then she could stop in at the fifth floor to check on Jon—and give him a report on the situation—on her way to the roof. And if they hadn't restored power by the time she got up there, Verity could still examine the base tower's exterior to see if she could *see* any damage.

At least the doors had automatically unsealed—with the net down she couldn't use the codes on her pad to unlock them—and she could reenter through the same side door she'd so recently exited. Making her way along the back corridors with her pad supplementing the emergency lighting, she reached the transmission room and shoved the wide door open, shined her makeshift flashlight to study the scene in front of her without entering. And her heart briefly stopped.

In the center of the small space a four-foot-high pedestal stood empty. The square black box, which normally sat atop it, lay broken on the hard surface of the floor below. As far as she could tell, the separate panels which were the six sides that formed the box remained intact but had cracked apart to reveal the dark gray sphere inside. She shivered.

No techie or expert herself, someone else would have to examine the panels to discover any damage and make any necessary repairs. What Verity knew —and she was one of a very few privy to the secret— was what that sphere contained. Though any of the techs who worked on the power system understood the vast amount of energy the thing radiated. Much of which was beamed up to batteries on satellites as far more was generated than the FURC could use or store. Enough excess energy to turn them all to ash if those panels didn't absorb it all.

Since she wasn't dead already, something must have happened to stop the sphere's discharge—that thought was almost as frightening, as it would continue creating power on the inside. She didn't know how much the sphere could contain before it caused unfathomable disaster. Would it explode?

She didn't know that either, only that whatever happened it would destroy the world.

Taking a deep breath, Verity regained her poise as she remembered the world wouldn't end, not for a long time anyway. Her husband had not let much about the future slip, but one thing that was evident from what she *had* heard was that this time she was living through—ahead of her own native era—would be considered distant history, at least from Turner's point-of-view. Meaning there was a far future. And he'd been adamant that it couldn't be changed even as he insisted people had free will and could choose what to do.

Well, she hadn't been interested in the abstract theory. She'd wanted to know what the future held and gleaned as much as she could from the little he had said. Which hadn't been a lot. But Verity knew the earth still existed in that future, so a disaster on the scale she was scared of would not occur.

A low moan interrupted her thoughts. Shifting the light from her pad to the corner showed the tech who was supposed to be on duty here sitting on the ground next to his workstation with a gash bleeding on the side of his head.

Closing her eyes briefly to recall the room's layout, she then walked carefully around the black box and over to the opposite corner, where a small cabinet held assorted supplies. Including a first-aid kit. Grabbing that and continuing her circuit, assessing what damage she could see along the way, she came to the groggy man and helped him sit up, supported by his back against the wall. Then she took a hydrogen peroxide wipe from the kit and cleaned the laceration on the side of his head. Slapped a Neosporin patch on it and then a square gauze bandage. He gave her a weak smile in return.

"Don't try to talk, just rest and recuperate." He obviously wasn't in any shape to help her, and Verity wasn't qualified to determine what repairs needed to be made. Much less to fix anything.

But she'd seen cracks in two of the transmitters on the walls. And she knew those would need to be repaired first—as she understood it, the energy discharged by the sphere was absorbed then converted by the panels that formed the sides of the box, then they sent electricity to the four larger panels placed on each wall. As well as to one on the ceiling.

She swung the beam from her pad up and tried to examine the panel above, but it was too high and remained obscured in shadow. At least she'd gotten a good look at the base of the pedestal, and that appeared undamaged. It also absorbed electricity, directly from the bottom of the box, and fed it into the node that powered everything in this building.

Still, that would have to be thoroughly checked, as well as the five transmitter panels, and all necessary repairs made. And any mending those smaller panels required, the ones comprising the black box.

All of which work would need to be done before the sphere could be reactivated—always assuming they could figure out how to do that, while reassembling the box around it without irradiating everyone. Assuredly special equipment would be needed to handle things during that last delicate step.

Verity and this half-conscious tech didn't have a hope of managing that. And she couldn't call those who could, wasn't sure where she could find them if she dared head out to look. She'd have to hope that those techs realized the power being out meant they were needed here, that they were able to come, and that they were already heading this way.

In the meantime, she should climb the stairs to the fifth floor to make sure Jon was alright and give him the unpalatable facts. Only, one of the techies, whose help they needed so badly, could walk in any moment. And she'd have to be here to see that they understood exactly what needed to be done. And to warn them.

Chapter 6

Worrying What May Come

9:45 p.m. Friday, May 27th
At the FURC main gates

SGT. TIM MACTIERNY scowled as he gestured at the two guards to get on with rolling the gate section of the security fence back to let in the four people waiting patiently on the other side. The middle-aged woman and three kids had approached timidly and with no attempt at stealth. And didn't even appear to be armed.

How they'd managed to reach the FURC gate he couldn't imagine, unless this was some sort of trick. Or a miracle. MacTierney wondered which. Hoped it was the latter, but he was alert to the possibility it would be the former, that they'd have to defend the compound against another attack.

According to the administration's rules, any attempt by outsiders to force their way into the FURC should be repelled by the minimum amount of force necessary to prevent entry. The same went for anyone who tried to sneak in. When it came to those in the final stages of a Gravity Bug infection, that usually meant shooting them in the head or heart. And Tim didn't mind putting those poor creatures out of their misery. Not after Mathers.

But anyone who approached either of the gates peacefully, asking for asylum, had to be allowed inside. The guards would turn them over to Security, and then they'd be *their* problem.

MacTierney had reported this new group of refugees already, but he wasn't sure how long it would take to send someone to pick these people up, since David was the one scheduled to handle that process this evening and he'd just taken a couple of newbies in not that long ago. Paul wasn't on call tonight, no doubt busy with council affairs, and Tim wasn't going to bother him. Even if Macklin might've appreciated the interruption.

Procedure was for the guards to search the new people—for weapons, which for the most part would be returned eventually, after they'd been fully vetted by Security, and for contraband. Like illegal drugs, which would be confiscated and destroyed, or other unsavory material. Notes about those things would be placed in the person's file. Then they were Security's concern.

Tim didn't know how they dealt with those people, and he was glad he didn't have to. He certainly didn't like the idea that individuals who'd have such items in their possession were allowed inside at all, much less accepted as citizens. But the council had decided the rules.

At least those were straightforward, made MacTierney's job simple enough. And if any of the new citizens caused trouble, Chief Nelson would be sure to take care of them one way or another.

Forcing his attention back to his own task, Tim waved the woman and her kids into the buffer zone and gestured at the pair of guards who weren't busy closing the gate in the security fence to start searching the mother. Not that MacTierney thought these people would be carrying contraband, but he wasn't about to take any chances. Which reminded him to move his gaze back past the gate and into the night. Out there in the shadows and among the trees, that would be where an attack would come from—if this was a trick, which he doubted. But Lt. Miles always preached continual vigilance.

It was when you let your guard down that trouble pounced, something she should know all about. Tim thought she was awesome. Then blushed as he realized that Grace might consider such admiration a betrayal of sorts, of his feelings for her, except she seemed to admire Lt. Miles even more than he. She had even transferred from Security to the guards to work under her.

Well, Grace claimed internal security work had become boring, as the motive for her move, that she wanted a job which provided more opportunities to shoot at something—or someone. To use the sniper rifle she cherished more than most people did their pets.

Shaking his head, MacTierney was glad that as a sergeant he had the option of carrying only a hand-gun for a sidearm. Of course, he wasn't a great shot like Grace.

Likely never would be, no matter how much Lt. Miles made him practice at the range. With so little improvement to show for it. Thankfully Grace liked him in spite of all his shortcomings and lack of am-bition.

And if he couldn't work with her on his team, at least the lieutenant had scheduled them to work the same shift, so he and Grace could spend a fair bit of their time off together. That meant she was on duty with only one other guard as her partner, patrolling the buffer zone. Though at the moment she should be temporarily stationed at the back gate.

Forcing his mind once again back to his job, he saw the security fence had been secured and waved the pair of guards to slide open the main gate while the other two finished going through the little family's meager belongings. While his eyes darted back and forth between the four being searched and that area beyond the fence from which the enemy might attack. Would, eventually, if not now.

He was aware the gate behind him was halfway open—had halfway turned at an oncoming rumble—when the ground beneath his feet threw him up into the air. The world whirled. Spun around in his peripheral vision. And roared in his ears.

Then his back hit the pavement, pain searing in so many places as broken bits of asphalt jabbed into different areas across his body. And his mind went blank.

For a long moment everything seemed to stop—extended silence in the pitch-black night and only a lot of agony to tell him he was still alive. Then sight and sound flooded his senses and time started flowing again as a wail crashed through the quiet, lights threw back the shadows, and MacTierney heard his guards cursing. He didn't call them on it.

Refraining from joining them though, he swore silently instead as he sat up and surveyed the situation. A couple of fence posts torn out of the ground had the top sagging outward toward the earth, even brushing the grass at the lowest point. All the razor wire would still cause most invaders to hesitate, but not the truly desperate. Or anyone in the later stage of the Gravity Bug infection.

The other guards were all on their feet, and Tim stood too, though his injuries made him wince as he pushed himself up. The one kid—he looked four or five—continued to cry until his mother, sitting down on the ground next to him, hugged him close.

Glancing back, MacTierney saw the gate standing open and shouted out, "Defensive positions two by two in the buffer zone." And watched the grumbling guards unsling their rifles and form up, into a slanted square facing away from the compound.

That would do for now, but he would need reinforcements. Pulling the pad out of his shirt pocket, he found the FURCSnet down, unable to connect to HQ. He looked back past the main gate and saw the lamplights lining the street were out, meaning power everywhere was out, and he thanked whoever had seen that the spotlights around the gate had battery backup. At least they could see here.

But the security fence might be down anywhere along the perimeter. And as long as power was out, no one would get alerts sent from the sensors in the buffer zone. The two pairs of guards patrolling that area couldn't monitor the entire length, so a breach might go undetected. And the wall wouldn't be that hard to scale. But MacTierney couldn't do anything about that yet.

The front and back gates in the wall were where they'd have to concentrate their defense for now, as the two easiest points of entry into the compound—and he couldn't even do that properly without more men here. It would be worse at the back gate where only Grace and that idiot Wagner were stationed.

Tim couldn't check on Grace until communications were restored. Or call for help. No, he had to focus on what he *could* do.

Limping over to where the mother still sat with the kid clutched in her arms and her other children huddled around her, MacTierney looked them over and saw scrapes and cuts. But the boy had stopped howling. And none of them appeared to be in great pain. "Can you stand? Walk?" Emergency medical supplies were kept in the guard station on the other side of the wall.

The middle-aged woman nodded, started to use her left arm to push herself up, and gave a sharp cry as she collapsed back. Breathing raggedly she let go of the child she'd been holding in her right arm and used that to cradle her left. "I think it's broken."

He helped her to her feet. "Come with me. And I'll see what we can do about that."

As he led her through the wide gap where they'd pulled the front gate back, he noticed the metal had been twisted and wondered if it would slide into the wall and lock like it was supposed to. Probably not, but he bet it would be an easy fix. At least once they could get someone here to work on it.

The security fence would likely be easy to repair as well, once it was daylight, and they had men who could fix the damage, and enough guards to protect them while they worked.

At the hut used as a base by the squad assigned to the main gate, MacTierney found a sling and slid it gently around the woman to hold her broken arm and cleaned and bandaged all her cuts and scrapes, and the children's, ignoring his own.

"That's the best we can do for you here. I know you'd probably like to just sit and rest, but you need further medical attention." And Security needed to process them, but that would have to wait, as would getting them to the clinic. "Go as slow as necessary to be safe, but follow me."

He left the hut and started down the sidewalk—it looked mostly intact—in the direction of the guard headquarters. Thankfully that wasn't far, and there would be more first-aid supplies waiting. As well as someone with more experience using them.

But more urgent than taking care of these newbies' needs was reporting to Chief Cameron. Asking him to send all available guards to the gates. These people could receive further treatment as well as be kept secure at HQ, but MacTierney would be happy to leave those decisions to the Chief—as long as the man ordered plenty of reinforcements to proceed to the back gate immediately.

He had to go a lot slower than he wanted. Sore as he might be, he still easily outpaced the family he was leading and kept having to stop until they could catch up. He tried to be patient and understanding as they gradually made their way, but his mind was filled with worry for Grace. Even knowing how well she could take care of herself.

The headquarters building was dark when they approached the door, but at least inside the dim red emergency lighting helped. Though the absence of a guard on duty in the lobby didn't. Nor did a shouted curse coming from further inside the building.

MacTierney left them sitting there in hard plastic chairs, though they seemed relieved for a chance to rest regardless. And marched down the corridor toward Chief Cameron's office.

He found five guards—the four on duty and stationed at HQ and another who was off duty but presumably close enough to get here swiftly—crowding the anteroom and muttering in low voices. And the door to the inner office standing open. From within another strong oath boomed forth like an explosion going off. Chief Cameron, cursing again.

MacTierney nodded at the assembled guards as he pushed through to stand in the doorway. Inside, the man himself was leaning back in his chair with a deep scowl and his right leg stretched across the top of the desk. That leg had already been splinted, and now the Chief's secretary was wrapping it in gauze.

The middle-aged woman in civilian clothes took the time to glare at Tim, then went back to her work and spoke over her shoulder. "Looks like his femur has been fractured. They should be taking him over to the clinic, but he insists on staying here. In command, as if there's anything he can do."

"There are four newcomers waiting in the lobby who need medical attention. Maybe you could help them once you've finished with the Chief. I need to give him my report."

The woman harrumphed and yanked the end of the bandage tight before taping it down and causing Cameron to bellow wordlessly. MacTierney waited a moment so the man could hear him, then explained the situation.

"...so I suggest sending two guards, one in each direction along the buffer zone"—and Tim intended to be one of them—"to inspect both the wall and the fence for damage, and join with the regular patrols. They can all finish up at the back gate and reinforce the guards already there." Then he'd feel Grace was alright. Then he'd know.

Chapter 7

When You Lose Heart

9:45 p.m. Friday, May 27th
First Councilor's Office, Community Hall

CAROLINE SMILED WARMLY as she met the gaze of each of the eight citizens in her office, shook their hands one by one as they started for the door. "Just remember, Councilor Fox represents the largest businesses in the community and is beholden to the established concerns. Individual entrepreneurs like yourselves struggling to build small businesses, however, have different needs. And you understand now how I've been working hard on your behalf."

Approval glinted in every eye as they all nodded and thanked her for her efforts, then moved toward the hall. Most, or maybe all, would vote for her in a year when they had the next election. More importantly, they might decide before then to switch their representation registration, from business sector to general community member. And that would lessen Alvin's leverage in the Council.

After shepherding the last guest out, Caroline's assistant Carmen closed the door and consulted her pad. "That's the last meeting that was on your schedule for this evening, but a few of the other councilors are still in the building. If you want to see them before you go home..."

Caroline started shaking her head, happy at the thought of finally ending the day, when the building itself began shaking. Suddenly dizzy and disoriented, she stumbled and fell. She somehow caught the back of one of the chairs as she crashed to the floor, pulled it down on top of her.

Thankfully it wasn't too heavy. As soon as everything stopped rattling she was able to shove it off. Power was out, but the emergency lighting was sufficient to show Carmen struggling to her knees near the door. Bruised but otherwise uninjured, Caroline managed to stand as her assistant searched around for the pad she'd dropped.

Clutching the workpad to her chest, the woman used the doorknob as an anchor and got to her feet. "The net's down, mam."

"First things first. We should be evacuating the building—it might not be sound, and there could be aftershocks." It had been a long time since they had a crisis here, and people would be confused, scared. A lot of them, anyway. "It would help if you opened the door, Carmen."

With wide eyes the woman shook her head and then nodded, then turned and opened the door and darted out into the hall. Clearly rattled.

Caroline dusted herself off as she followed, saw her assistant murmuring to the eight citizens who'd just left her, who hadn't made it very far. "Let's get a move on, folks. Turn right down that hallway and out the back door." She had to chivvy them along—bathed in hazy red illumination they looked washed out and weary. Whoever was out in front turned as she'd directed. "That's right. Keep going out of the building until you're well clear."

Another half dozen or so were approaching from the other direction, merging with her group, crowding together in the short stretch of corridor that led to the exit. Two councilors, Paul and Tracy, among them. There should be more. They should be—and hopefully were—evacuating through the front doors and out the main entrance. She should send someone to check.

A few moments later they were all outside turning back to stare at the dark hulk of the Community Hall, though it looked the same as always. Caroline swiveled back around and herded them a bit farther away, just in case. Then turned back again, and her gaze landed on the much larger, darker mass of the Administration building beyond.

Miles.

She grabbed Carmen's arm. "Take care of these here." Without waiting for the response, she started stumbling across the grass toward the northern end of the Hall, weaving her way around the people who still stood and stared. And once past the crowd, she found herself forced to go slow, had to squint down at the now uneven ground to pick out the most level path forward. In the direction she was headed.

The moon softly glowed somewhere behind her low on the horizon, but that gauzy illumination illuminated little. Out here was even darker than it had been inside with the emergency lighting.

"Caroline!"

She glanced back over her shoulder to see Paul—the tall, skinny student representative was coming after her—and kept going.

"You should have an escort. And I'm still working for Security." His voice grew more distant, and she knew she was leaving him behind.

Shaking her head she didn't bother to look back again. "I don't need it." And he would just slow her down. "But they need your help here."

And Miles needed her, or maybe it was just that she needed him, to see he was alright. Either way it was obvious where he'd be. The man never seemed to leave his office in administration unless he knew she'd be home, and he'd have known she was still at the Community Hall. In meetings, as usual.

Then bright lights flashed behind her, followed by the whine of an electric cart. And Paul pulled up alongside, grinning. "I can get you wherever you're going sooner *and* safer."

Caroline automatically opened her mouth to reject the offer before realizing he was right. Paul had caught up to her, after all. "Alright." Since the cart was already matching her pace, she hopped into the passenger seat without difficulty. "To Admin."

He bumped the cart across the grass and circled around the building. And in the glare of the brights she saw a larger crowd, several dozen at least, milling around in the area in front of the steps up to the main entrance. She saw Jeffrey talking to someone, but not Fox. But she couldn't afford to worry where he might be or what he might be up to. Not now. A moment later they were swallowed by shadow, Paul turning the cart and bouncing it up onto a concrete walkway which would wind toward the Green.

With the headlights on bright, the way ahead of them stood in sharp relief to the black night around them as they glided on. Paul even accelerated a bit, though she felt sure she could walk almost as fast on what at first was a mostly level surface.

But she could only see the way so clearly thanks to the cart's lights, and the way wasn't clear. Cracks in the concrete began appearing more often and became larger as they traveled. Their rate of progress slowed as Paul eased back on the gas and occasionally was forced off the walkway and around a larger crack, too wide or too high for the cart's wheels.

Then the headlights flickered and began fading and died. Followed a moment later by the engine.

The cart coasted a few more feet to roll gently to a stop against another broken part of the pathway—but before it came to a complete halt, Caroline half-fell from her seat as she slid off and staggered three or four paces away. She knew they'd been rounding the southern end of the Green, from the murmuring of the masses she'd heard stranded in the dark park, so she pulled the pad from her purse and used it as a flashlight, started walking on a diagonal line toward the Admin building. And moved as fast as she could under the circumstances.

Paul yelled at her to wait, which order of course she ignored, and soon he'd caught up and added the illumination from his own pad to help in navigating their way through the dark and across the grass. As they stalked along, he tried talking to her.

"I'm surprised the power isn't back on yet. Surprised it went out in the first place, if I'm honest. It shouldn't, not all over the compound like this. And crippling the carts and shutting down the net. This is a disaster. I mean..."

Caroline sighed. It was a fair question, likely an important one as well, but she didn't dare divert the attention necessary to consider it. Just walking was enough of a challenge, and keeping up a good pace. "Ask someone who knows about those things, Paul. But later, if everything hasn't been fixed by the time you find them."

"I've only studied the details of our wireless energy transmission system on a pad, but while all the shaking might've broken one or more of the panels, it must've been really bad at Admin, to have broken every one. I thought that's why you're headed there actually. It's not, though." Half a question.

She stumbled as the import of what he had been saying hit her. "Admin is where all that power stuff is?" Where whatever it was had gone wrong.

"That's where the energy source is, where those transmission panels I assume were destroyed in the earthquake are."

His words brought a vision of total devastation, vast ruin to her mind. But that had to be on the inside. They'd gotten close enough now to see details amongst the shadows cloaking the building, and no damage was visible. Yet.

Such a gentleman—as they approached the back entrance Paul dashed ahead of her to open the door and held it for her. Stepping through and scanning what she could see from the back of the large lobby, everything appeared normal. But there wasn't light enough to really tell.

And she didn't have time to make any closer inspection. Seeing the door to one of the corner stairwells standing open, Caroline ran through, began to climb the steps. She thought she heard Paul yelling something behind her but wasn't sure.

Unable to stop or turn back for that, she rushed on, started to reach for the railing to help her climb faster before she saw it had broken lose, further up, from the brackets holding it to the wall. Noticed an almost invisible crack running across the plaster.

Still, not as much damage as she'd feared. And while there might be more serious problems underneath the surface, she didn't think the building was about to fall down around her ears. She would find Miles, and he'd be alright.

Maybe a little shaken. She was herself, but had no time to count her bruises. Several steps past the second-floor landing meant almost three flights left to go. The inconvenience of no electricity.

She could use some of her daughter's hardiness at the moment—Caroline knew herself soft, but also understood there was little she could do about it, at the moment. And once power was restored and life had returned to normal, she doubted she'd have the motivation to make any changes. Developing skills such as Kat had took a lot of discipline and commitment. And time. Things Caroline lacked. But once she'd found Miles, she wouldn't care about that.

And if bruises like hers were the worst anybody had suffered, they'd been fortunate indeed.

Her muscles protested as she reached the fifth-floor landing, but relief that she'd made it up all five flights washed away the momentary fatigue. And so far she'd seen only a few more faint cracks.

But then she pushed through the stairwell door and stepped out into a corridor and saw more, went into the large outer office and stopped and stared at all the disarray. Pictures knocked off walls, various papers and equipment thrown from desktops to the floor, and drawers half-slid out, hanging awkwardly in the air. "Miles!"

Weaving her way around the desks and over the mess the quake had left, she realized that's all it was —one huge confusion of clutter. It would have to be cleaned up. And the building itself would no doubt require some minor repairs. "Miles!"

Maybe he'd headed home early, even if it would have been unusual behavior for him. But then, he'd been unpredictable, back in the past.

Still, she continued working her way around to the heavy oak door on the far side with its engraved inscription—*FURC Director Jonathan Miles.* Which stood firmly shut. And she couldn't hear any sound of life within.

Since she was already there anyway though, she turned the knob and pushed the door open. Found Miles lying on the floor in the middle of the room, a filing cabinet fallen across his legs, and with his face covered in blood. Then he moaned, softly.

Caroline dropped to her knees and tried to push the filing cabinet off him, but it was too heavy. And she didn't have the strength.

His eyes fluttered open, then a weak smile tried to form at the corners of his mouth. "You came."

"Of course I did. But I can't get this thing off of you, and I can't call for help." Not with her pad but with her voice. "Paul! In here!" And she did have a strong pair of lungs. "Someone! Anyone! We need help!" Though the building had felt empty and lifeless to her, there should be somebody.

Miles started to shake his head. But she caught it in her hands, held his face still with her left while her right dug a handkerchief out of her purse—she used it to tenderly wipe away the blood. Out of one eye and then from the long cut across his forehead.

"Thanks, Care." It wasn't much more than a feeble croak, but it warmed her heart.

"I hate to leave you here alone again, but I have to get help. At least find Paul—he brought me here, and with his help we can lift this thing off you. And we'll bring back a first-aid kit, so I can start bandaging you while he goes and fetches a med tech. Must be one around somewhere."

Miles met her eye with a fixed look. "No, please don't leave, dear. It's too late anyway. And I'm not in any pain, not anymore."

His voice weakening with each word, she had to lean closer to hear. Then wished she hadn't. "Don't say that. Once we get you proper medical attention you'll be alright—have you forgotten how fast we all heal now?"

"Help couldn't come soon enough." He sighed. "I can feel myself fading fast. I want you with me at the end, and there are things I have to say, so much I have to tell you. And not enough time."

"Shut up, Miles. You're going to be fine. You're not going to leave me here. Not going to make me a widow." Caroline felt herself getting mad. Growing angrier by the moment. "Don't you dare."

He ignored her. "It'll be up to you to lead them now, to carry on my vision." What did he think she was doing as First Councilor? "You'll be better at it that I ever was, but there are things you don't know yet. Verity knows everything. Listen to her, get the details. She can't guide the community the way you can, but you need to work with her. And trust..."

His voice trailed away, disappeared completely, even as she moved her ear to his mouth to catch the last word. There were no more after that. And not a breath either. Laying the side of her head down onto his chest, all she heard was silence.

Then a faint wuffling and mewling started. She couldn't understand what was making such a pitiful noise at first. But it was her, crying. Weeping softly and trying to breathe, as her tears gradually soaked her husband's shirt.

Part Two

Committed Action

Chapter 8

Turning Things Around

9:55 p.m. Friday, May 27th
FURC Detention Center

SARA SHOVED THE staff room door shut, then bolted it from the inside to cover her rear. Marigold might rouse any minute and come after her. Or one of the others.

A quick scan of the room sufficed to inform her it was empty—a large oval table sat in the middle of the space, with several chairs ranged around, but no people. Not a surprise since the scream she'd heard came from the break room next door, but good that she found it unoccupied. One of the male prisoners might've made their way in here.

This was where the officers detailed to work the detention center operated out of—where they began and ended their shift anyway, and spent a few minutes tapping reports into their pads. What free time they had was usually spent snacking and chatting in the break room. Just through a doorless entry off to her left.

Sara had made a split-second decision when the cry for help seized her attention. Rather than try to barge into the break room through the hallway door and straight into an unknown situation, she decided to go through the connecting conference room. The open entryway would let her move closer and assess what she'd be walking into first.

Approaching the opening from the left side, she saw Michelle poised with pepper spray aimed in the direction of the door. Dropping to a crouch, hoping the dim lighting and deep shadows would help hide her movement, Sara scuttled over to the other side. Looked up to see Greg with a bloody face and facing off against a guy who looked much larger. Wearing one of the bright orange jumpsuits. And an expression of hate.

Before the thug could continue his assault, Sara rolled through into the break room and came up on the man's right side, surprising him. He tried turning a forward lunge at Greg into a vicious backhand at her head, but she was already spinning into him, capturing his arm, and breaking his balance. Locking his elbow and shoulder, she leveraged him down to the ground and kept turning, plowed his face into the thin carpet covering the cement floor. And with as much force as she could manage.

Wrenching his shoulder and making him moan in pain, she rued not having zip-ties with which she could restrain him, but she wasn't Security anymore. She wore the same sort of orange outfit at this thug. Branding her as a fellow detainee.

She tried to smile at Michelle while keeping the prisoner pinned, but the petite officer didn't appear very reassured. "Can you zip-tie this guy? I should check the kitchen to make sure there aren't more of them coming through."

The other woman peered back at her, obviously considering the situation, then reached into a pouch on her belt—with the hand that wasn't wielding the pepper spray—and took out a handful of the plastic straps. Came forward and handed them to Sara. "I think you may end up needing to zip-tie more guys. And I have to take care of Greg."

Michelle crossed to the far wall and took down a first-aid kit as Sara got her first good look at the new officer's face. A split lip and a bloody nose said he'd taken one or two heavy blows. And the way his jaw hung loose explained why he had remained speechless so far.

Reaching down and grabbing the other wrist of the troublemaker under her, Sara zip-tied his hands behind him and left him lying on the floor, then ran across the room and into the cramped kitchen.

It only took her a minute to see the space didn't contain any more wandering prisoners, but a spraying sound directed her attention to the water which was running onto the floor in front of the industrial sized sink.

She swore under her breath, but she couldn't do anything about that. She did bolt the door opening into the corridor.

Back in the break room she told Michelle about the kitchen as she watched the woman clean Greg's face, bandage his lip and nose, and wrap gauze over his head to hold his jaw firmly shut. Seemed the kid would continue the silent act for a while.

Then the heavily bandaged—and hopefully well medicated—Greg ground out some words through a barely moving mouth. "I'll take care of the kitchen. Know how to shut the water off."

Sighing, Sara started toward the door out of the break room before Officer Mori gave her any orders she wouldn't want to follow. "Bolt this behind me." And then she slipped through into the hall, shutting the door softly and scanning in every direction. But as yet there were no visible threats.

Being a newbie, Greg wasn't up to dealing with a riot, and while Michelle was thoroughly trained, she would be in over her head as well. Sara wouldn't be able to handle half a dozen violent offenders either, but at least she wasn't an officer any longer. Didn't have to play nice. Not that she'd played by the rules very well when she'd been in Security—a big part of her problem—but the other two would be hampered by an inherent unwillingness to go no-holds-barred the way Sara could. The way she found natural.

And to think, before she began copying Kat, she had been a spoiled little princess.

Most of the prisoners had probably fled already —unlocked doors being an irresistible temptation— and some may have scaled the security fence and be roaming the compound by now. There was nothing Sara could do about that.

And a majority of the detainees here weren't so bad. Unfortunately that would make them obvious victims for the more violent inmates.

So while Michelle and Greg would've focused on evacuating the building—probably should be getting out themselves—Sara could concentrate on bringing down the worst actors. That was a more immediate danger than a potentially unsound structure.

And she already knew where she would find the most menacing—after herself—female detainee. So she stood to one side as she threw open the door into the women's ward.

Marigold was moaning but already trying to get to her feet, and Sara sped down the wide hall to stop her, pushed the woman back down and zip-tied her hands. Marigold rolled onto one side and spat out a word that rhymed with witch, which Sara had heard far too often to be fazed by.

She gave the woman a wide grin as she checked the cells swiftly and confirmed all the other inmates had fled. Then returned to the back corridor.

Padding quickly through the resource rooms to the shower facilities, she found no one on either the women's or men's side, then braced herself and approached the open door to the men's ward. The one thug hadn't shut it behind him, but she hadn't seen another man around anywhere. Not yet. At least it seemed none of the others had decided to head back to the staff area.

But Michelle and Greg would both be safe now, behind those bolted doors. Sara worried what she'd find through this one—especially since she heard an argument echoing out.

She crouched low and peered around the frame of the door, saw four large guys shoving and shouting, and shuddered. Getting in the middle of a fight between them would be stupid, and she wasn't good enough to take them all on at the same time. Some creative tactics were called for.

Waving her hands in the air, she ran screaming onto the ward. "Fire! Get out while you can! Don't just stand there!" Kept running at them full tilt.

The two farthest from her turned, took off like a shot toward the other door, and dove through to the lobby without a backward glance. But the other two turned toward her. And advanced. From the looks on their faces, they couldn't care less about any fire—supposing the troglodytes had even understood.

But however tough they might be, neither was a trained fighter. They crowded together, got in each other's way as they came at her, while she kept running right at them. When the guy on her right tried to grab one of her hands, she caught his instead and twisted his wrist to plow him further into the other. Stomped her heel through the side of his knee, sent him collapsing into his friend.

Or not a friend. He shoved the one who wailed in pain now away so he could seize her, but she was already ducking and driving a fist into his groin and crashing a knee down onto his instep. He howled—and still managed to wrap his sweaty hands around her neck.

Digging her chin into the back of a thumb, Sara bent her head under that hand—almost passing out from the pressure—as she dropped further. Forcing his grip to weaken. Then she was on her butt, shoving her foot up into his crotch and rolling backward to throw him over her as he lost his hold.

The other guy was cursing as he struggled to his feet. Panting, she staggered over and slammed him back to the ground, rolled him over and zip-tied his hands. Making her way back over to where she had tossed his 'friend', she saw he was unconscious and bleeding from a bad knock on the head where it had hit the floor. He might die if he couldn't get treated soon, but she wouldn't lose any sleep over it.

She could fetch Michelle, who had considerable medical training—instead, she zip-tied his hands too and started for the lobby, gently feeling her throat.

As brief as it had been, he'd squeezed more than hard enough to leave a bruise. And her breath felt a little raspy. Another second or two without oxygen and she wouldn't have been able to keep fighting.

That had been far too close for comfort, but she couldn't stop now. Only four down and no idea how many of the remaining twenty or so inmates would need to be taken down, how many were out there in the Yard and ready to cause trouble. Assuming they hadn't started already.

Maybe it's time to stop trying to be a hero.

Chapter 9

Taking Risks

9:55 p.m. Friday, May 27th
Outside the Administration Building

PAUL WATCHED CAROLINE hurry on ahead of him as he followed more cautiously, scanning his surroundings and seeing no threats. Rushing could cause trouble that would trip you up. Go slow, keep it smooth and steady, and you'd get there sooner in the end. That's what Chief Nelson and Lt. Miles had taught him after he signed up to Security, and what he'd found to be true. Though he'd only started applying the principle consistently after Sara had shot him. That day had changed his life in several ways. Put him on the council as the representative for the FedU student body. Made him a hero to some. And ended an awkward relationship.

Entering Admin through the door Caroline had just gone in, he found the lobby empty. Even in the dim red emergency lighting, he would've seen her if she'd been there. Closing his eyes, he stopped. Listened carefully.

The rustle of her dress faintly echoing out of the open stairwell told him where she was. Opening his eyes, he walked over to the bottom step and shouted up at her. "Wait! We should check out things down here first." He'd come along to protect her, but she was making it difficult. And he had a responsibility to the wider community, to all its citizens, so he refrained from following her up the stairs.

Besides, either she hadn't heard him calling out or had ignored him. With a sigh, he waved the light from his pad ahead of him as he roamed around the back end of the lobby. Definitely empty, and not so much damage as he'd expected.

Perhaps the quake hadn't been as bad as all the shaking had made it feel or as devastating as all the churned up ground and cracked walkways had suggested. On the other hand, power was still out.

Up front and off to either side were some small conference rooms, a little café, and other facilities—but pretty much everything here, even the reception desk, was shut down by six—and back here he knew there were supply closets and such. All of which he could check out, would need to be gone through.

But also located down a side hall he had already started toward was the wireless power transmission room, the heart of the FURC's electrical system, and probably where whatever problem had plunged the compound into darkness would be found. Hopefully, people were working there even now, doing everything they could to bring the power back. Though if so, they were being awfully quiet.

Whether techs were fixing the fault or none had made their way here yet, Paul knew enough to help, and restoring power remained the most urgent need of the community. Which meant he should check it out first.

Beams of light flashed around the dark through the little window in the wide door, proving someone was in there before he pushed his way into the room and recognized Verity. The deputy director stood in the middle of the room near the central pedestal, on her toes, stretching her hand as high as she could to play the light from her pad across the ceiling. With her back to him.

Sitting unsteadily on the floor and leaning back against the wall was a uniformed tech—presumably the man who'd been on duty here—wearing a bulky bandage over the side of his head. He had been observing Verity but, noticing Paul's entrance, turned his attention to the new arrival. And that in its turn alerted her to his presence.

"Paul." She dropped to her heels as she turned to greet him, shifting the beam of light to shine into his eyes. "I suppose you could be useful. Anyway, I can't stay here, but you can. Now that you're here, I can let you explain the situation to whichever techs show up." She shook her head. "They'd better show up soon."

Paul shielded his face with an arm. "What's the situation? You haven't explained anything."

With a sigh she lowered the light to shine at his feet. "And I'll have to take the time to fill you in, or else you won't be able to explain everything to whoever arrives to fix this."

"Let's start with why the power's out. You know what the problem is?" He let his arm drop.

She stepped to one side and shifted the beam to illuminate the empty top of the pedestal, then down to play over a black box that lay broken on the floor below it. And a dark gray sphere still half inside the box.

"That metal ball contains the power supply, *the highly unstable power supply*, for the FURC. And it must've stopped radiating energy automatically. Or else we'd all be dead." She peered at his face. "Have you any idea how much power it generates?"

He nodded. "Enough to provide the compound all the power it requires." More than enough to kill anyone in the room.

Verity blinked at him. "Far more than that—the transmission panel on the ceiling sends the surplus electricity to a receiver on the roof. And an antenna beams all that power to batteries orbiting in space."

On satellites, he supposed. "So it will need special handling once we can turn it on again, but I assume the box will need to be repaired first."

"And the transmission panels on the wall. Two or three cracks in those, that I was able to find. The one that's the base the box sits on looks alright, but an expert will need to examine it to be certain, and I can't see the one on the ceiling well enough. They'll all have to be fixed, and the repairs double checked before turning the sphere back on. Though I'm not sure anyone knows how to do that."

"What do you mean, no one knows?"

She shrugged. "The professor who designed the system said it was beyond our ability to understand how it worked. At least when it came to the sphere, and the panels that make up the box too, I think."

"Are you trying to tell me there's nothing we can do to restart the power source?"

"No, not at all. Though it may take the experts a bit of time to figure it out. I can't even tell you how or why it shut off—though I'm certainly glad it did." Her face looked grim. "But one thing I do know is—the power is still being generated inside the sphere. It's just not being released through the shell."

Paul wanted to swear. If all that energy continued building up inside the thing...

Verity coughed. "The techs responsible for this will make their way here just as fast as they can, I'm sure. You'll have to wait and explain all this to them when they arrive, because I can't. I've got too many other things to see to." She went around him to the door. "I'm sure I can count on you."

And then she was gone, leaving Paul at a loss on his own. Except for the one injured tech. Who was struggling to stand, using the workstation in the far corner to help him to his feet. Maybe the man could answer a few questions.

Paul crossed the room, giving the sphere and its box a wide berth, then lent an arm to the tech. "Are you sure you shouldn't be sitting down?"

The man shook his head, but slowly and gently. "I'm recovering pretty fast—nothing but a knock on the head, no concussion she said. And I don't want to just sit on my butt." And he sounded coherent.

"Well, I don't want to just stand around waiting and doing nothing." Particularly when there was no way to say when those other techs would show up—or if they could. "She said she found some cracks in those panels on the wall—you have any idea how to repair them?"

The man grinned. "Had an in-service on that a couple years back. Might be a bit rusty with the details, but I can refresh my memory by going through the manual."

Paul returned that grin. "Well, if there's a manual..." He could probably help make those repairs—only, with the net down how could he download the instructions to his pad? "You already have all those files on your workpad."

But the tech shook his head again, then nodded at the drawers built into the workstation he was still leaning against. "Everything's been printed and put in binders."

Naturally they would keep a hard copy of those instructions—which would be required if the power ever went out—on hand for reference. And how often had Paul mocked the Council's use of paper records in binders? The ones they hauled out anytime they argued about FURC policies. Though the practice wasn't supported by the same rationale that the power techs had. "So I can read through those, then give you a hand if you need it."

"If more techs haven't shown up by the time I'm ready to start. She may have found a couple cracks, but first we should both go over all the panels carefully to make sure we've found them all." He gazed up at the ceiling. "We'll have a tough job inspecting that one, though."

Paul nodded. "The cleaners have a supply closet down the hall, and the maintenance men a workroom. Should be able to find something we can use in one of those. I'll go take a look, and you start examining the wall panels. Alright?"

The man let go his hold on the workstation and straightened. "Makes sense to me. Just don't leave me alone too long."

Was this place giving the man the creeps or was he worried he might pass out? "Take it slow and be methodical. We can't afford to make a mistake. By the way, I don't even know your name." And he had to call the guy something if they were going to work together.

"I'm Chris. And of course I know who you are."

Paul felt a faint flush, but it shouldn't show, between the red glow and all the shadows. "So, Chris. You're sure you—we—can do this?"

"The light from our pads is bright enough. And we can use them to measure any cracks we find and record the location and dimensions. Then whoever does the repairs will know what they need to do."

Apparently the tech hoped someone else would show up to do that job. Well, Paul would appreciate that himself. But he wasn't going to count on it. So he waved and headed out into the hall.

He found the cleaners' supply 'closet' first—that term inapt for the huge space filled with shelves and stocked with sufficient supplies to last a year, in his estimation at least—but the best he could find was a step stool that would add a couple feet to his six and three inches. That might do, but he left it there and continued searching.

The workroom the maintenance men used was a bit larger, but it wasn't crammed full, so it felt much more spacious. And while there was a lot less in the way of supplies and equipment, he managed to find a six-foot ladder with folding support so it wouldn't need to be propped up against anything, which was exactly what he needed. With a steel frame it would be heavy, but he wouldn't have to carry it far, and it would surely be stable. And get him right up to the ceiling so he could closely inspect that panel.

Looping his arm under one of the rungs, he got a good grip on the side of the ladder and awkwardly carried it out and down the corridor and back to the power transmission room. Where he found Chris so absorbed in examining one of the panels he failed to notice Paul's return. At least the man wasn't having any trouble concentrating.

Paul coughed gently to avoid startling him, then set up the ladder close to the pedestal in the middle of the room, but on the opposite side of it from that sphere. Not that he was afraid of it. Or of an after-shock tossing him off while he inspected the ceiling panel. "I'm going to take a closer look at this box."

Chris turned and gaped. "That really should be left to the experts."

Kneeling down near the broken container, Paul shrugged. “They’re not here. And I am a Ph.D. student in theoretical physics.” And along the way he’d taken some courses in electrical engineering as well—the lab work he’d done for those wasn’t as good as having on-the-job experience, but it was better than nothing. “And I’m just going to look.”

He turned the beam from his pad onto the black box where it lay in pieces—shoving aside any worry over how long the battery would last the way he was using the pad—and carefully studied what he could see without touching anything.

Though the six matte black panels that made up the sides of the box appeared to be constructed of a carbon composite, he couldn’t be sure. And the little that was visible of their inside surface seemed to show silver-colored circuitry somehow embedded in whatever that material was. Which meant it probably hadn’t been damaged by crashing to the floor.

It would still have to be checked. But the better news, as he realized peering more closely, was those panels appeared to have come apart naturally. The ridges along some edges sliding out of fitted slots on others. It should be simple to reassemble the box.

That left the question of how to start the sphere releasing the power inside it again, and how to do it safely. Of course, if he could just figure out why the thing had shut off in the first place...

Standing and striding over to the workstation in the corner, he noticed Chris had returned to his examination of the panel on the one wall, and seemed to be studiously ignoring what Paul was doing. Absorbed in his work, hopefully.

Which was fine with Paul. He opened different drawers until he found what he wanted. A variable-spectrum radiation detector, a magnetometer, and a directional thermometer, as well as a pair of rubber gloves. Though he doubted those last would do any good.

He carried it all back to the middle of the room, then set about taking measurements. And as far as those instruments could tell, the sphere didn't have an electromagnetic field and emitted no radiation—not on any wavelength. It was totally inert and room temperature, even. Which worried him.

Verity hadn't said anything about *what* actually generated the power inside the sphere. He thought it would have to be some sort of fusion reactor, generating so much energy in such a small space. She'd been holding something back, anyway. That wasn't surprising—she and Director Miles both seemed secretive by nature.

But it made Paul uneasy, not knowing. Regardless, he donned the rubber gloves, then gently eased the sphere the rest of the way out of the opened box. The dark gray globe had a metallic sheen, weighed a lot less than he'd expected it to, and wasn't a proper sphere.

One part was level—the bottom, he presumed—with a protruding section to stand on...

Sudden understanding flashed in his mind. He carefully shifted the sphere to hold in his right hand and grabbed his pad with his left, used its illumination to inspect the base in more detail. And saw the flat solid circle he'd supposed it should stand up on would depress snugly into the bottom.

So sure was he now, Paul gently tested his theory by applying a little pressure with a gloved finger. The thing's own weight wouldn't be enough to push the base in, but he was willing to bet it had a spring release or the equivalent to have popped out so easily.

It was like a dead man's switch. If lifted up—or disturbed enough to roll off that base, such as by an earthquake—it would automatically turn off.

He didn't even need to know how *that* worked—he knew how to turn it back on, could see how to do that safely. Setting it down on the floor so it stayed with the base facing up, Paul stood and played light from his pad over the top of the pedestal. As Verity had told him, another panel was built into that, and it appeared undamaged.

And he could see how the bottom section of the box would fit perfectly flush with it. Then just slide the sides of the box into place and set the sphere in, base down.

Excited, he knelt on the floor again and studied the panel which had to be the top of the box, found a slightly rounded depression which would fit the top of the sphere. You would press that final panel into place to complete the box and simultaneously push the globe down, depressing the base. Which would switch the thing on safely, since all the panels would be in place to absorb the energy even if the power released immediately.

Paul forced himself to breathe slowly in order to calm down. First the transmission panels needed to be checked and repaired, and those repairs double-checked. Only then could he risk reassembling that box and restarting the power.

Aside from the danger to himself, and Chris, he also realized there would probably be broken nodes in buildings. Those receivers might start fires when the power came back on.

But they'd just have to deal with that then. Restoring power was too vital to wait until every node throughout the compound could be inspected. And repaired. With only the lights from their pads to go by, at least until daylight, which was still more than seven hours away.

And he couldn't waste any more time imagining what they'd need to do later. He stepped back over to the ladder so he could start examining the transmitter panel on the ceiling. They had lots of work to do yet.

Take it slow, make it steady and smooth, he told himself. *And you'll have the power back before you know it.*

Chapter 10
Dealing with Loss

10:05 p.m. Friday, May 27th
The top floor of the Administration Building

VERITY WEARILY CLIMBED the last step up to the fifth-floor landing and exited the stairwell too tired to call out to Jon—if he was still here. He likely would be. Frustrated, with the net down and not knowing what was going on, and waiting impatiently for her or someone to arrive and report.

Well, it had been a long day already even before the earthquake. And promised to be a longer night. With lots to do and little or no rest for anyone, so it would be necessary to conserve one's energy whenever possible. She had little reason to rush anyway, at least for the moment. She was waiting on others as well.

For the techs to get to the transmission room to restore power, most urgently. But that would take a while and give her plenty of time to check on Jon as well as the array on the roof, to make sure the servers could reboot properly, that the base tower would work, once they had the juice to run those things. If only Admin had a backup generator like the Medical Center...

But they barely had enough gas to run that for a couple hours, even after siphoning off fuel from the parked cars and trucks people rarely had any reason to use anymore. And the clinic needed it more than Admin anyway.

Besides, the experimental system they used now *was* their backup—or rather had been, for when the compound was cut off from the regional grid, or for when it failed on its own, whichever came first. The state had eventually shut off the electricity, but that grid had assuredly broken down by now. The FURC power supply wasn't supposed to fail.

Well, the power *source* couldn't. And presumably hadn't. But apparently no one—and she blamed herself here—had realized how vulnerable the actual transmission system was. Despite, or maybe due to, its cutting-edge technology.

Sighing, she rounded the square of desks in the center of the office suite, and her thoughts turned to Toby. Her chief assistant had headed home early to spend time with his family. How were they coping, without lights or communication or any of the many things that required power to run?

Then a faint cry came from the Director's office and drove everything else out of her mind. Jon was in pain.

She darted across the remaining space and into the room through the partially open door, but what she saw in the dim red haze was Miles stretched out on the carpet in front of his desk, one of his beloved cherrywood filing cabinets lying across his legs, and Caroline draped over his chest.

His wife must've been the one who cried—since Jon lay still and lifeless—she still moaned softly and wept onto her husband's shirt.

Verity very much feared her boss was dead.

Standing and staring for an unknown, unknowable length of time, her eyes suddenly popped open and she was swaying on her feet. Somehow she had briefly lost consciousness without realizing it at the time. Maybe she was in shock.

"Caroline." She called the woman's name softly several times before getting a response.

"Verity?" Then Caroline lifted her head, looked vaguely toward the door, her eyes overflowing pools with more tears yet to shed. "Is that you?" She was clearly out of it.

"Yes, it's me. Miles...?"

She shook her head. "He's gone. I got here too late, and there was nothing I could do, nobody here to help."

Verity couldn't tell if that was meant as criticism of her delayed arrival, but she took it as such, felt it deserved. "I'm sorry." She swallowed. "You're sure there's nothing we can do for him? Let me help you heave that cabinet off him."

Caroline shook her head, but when Verity had a good grip on the closest top corner, the other woman at least raised herself to a sitting position to give the thing a good shove on the other side. Enough to lift it off him, for Verity to get her shoulder under it and push it back upright. That earned her a tremulous smile.

But there'd been no sign of life from Jon, and it hit her that he really was gone, that what lay across the carpet now was only an empty husk.

After all they'd been through together, the hard work to plan the FURC project and see it started. If they hadn't completed it in time, there was plenty to do, to make the best of the mess, but he'd left her to clean it up on her own. Typical man.

"Come on, Caroline. There's nothing we can do for him now. You need to take care of yourself." At least clean herself up before going out in public.

Instead of rousing herself out of the stupor and rising to her feet, the other woman collapsed across

Jon's body and began weeping again. Verity wanted to slap her, but she didn't think that would actually accomplish anything. Still, her hand twitched.

"Alright, dear. Get all those tears out. But then think about your daughter, think what Miles would want. And remember there's a lot to do and a lot of people relying on you." Not for practical help. Only for 'leadership', but they could use some spine stiffening under the circumstances—even Verity herself—and that wasn't a skill in her own handbag.

Backing quietly out the door she left Caroline to her grief. She'd send someone here in a little while, to check on the woman, but that would have to be a person with tact and discretion. Thankfully she had plenty of time.

And more important things to see to at the moment. She didn't know how long it would be before techs who could fix the power system showed up, or how long it would take them to get it working again—too long, though. At least she could check the array on the roof, make sure the servers were ready to reboot. And hopefully fix any problems. So the net would come back online with the power and restore communications.

But she had so little energy left, and she blamed Jon's death for sapping what strength she'd had before finding him. Thankfully there was no reason to rush, but she did need to move. Somehow she managed to wander back over to the stairwell and trudge her way up to the door leading out onto the roof.

Silent air conditioners and giant spinning fans, pulling fresh air into the building, and vents to keep it all circulating—all those ugly protuberances were strewn around the roof. But in the very center rose several large steel boxes stacked like a small hill, and on top of the highest sat a couple of satellite dishes. She wasn't interested in those, though.

Two antennas stood pointing to the sky, one on either side of the pair of dishes. And they transmitted and received the radio signals which wirelessly connected the FURCSnet servers with the workpads and personal pads throughout the compound. Even with what little light her own pad could add—which was almost nothing at that distance—there were too many shadows to be sure, but in silhouette they appeared undamaged.

With a sigh she walked over to one of the bottom boxes, found a special key in her purse, and opened a panel set in its side. To one side of a small screen lots of little lights either blinked or glowed steadily. And most were green.

She had to peer closely and use the illumination from her pad to read the tiny writing under the one which blinked red. There was a fault in the parallel switch setup, the gadget that digitally directed bytes of data coming and going in and out of the communications relay. Until whatever was wrong had been fixed, the network couldn't function.

Setting that problem aside for the moment, she pushed a button below the screen to start the server self-diagnostic routine. The system had enough battery power to run that at least.

Then she shut the panel, though she didn't lock it, and walked around the array to another steel box and used the same key to unlock that. Pulling open one side revealed a dark cavity containing the parts of the relay. After taking a second to recall what the parallel switch looked like, she used the light of her pad again—grateful it hadn't run out of power yet—to find that.

Taking off the housing covering its guts, she saw several circuit boards had fallen out of the slots they should've been sitting in snuggly. She'd have to remove each one in turn and examine them closely to see if any had been damaged. She hoped not, as the repairs would need to be done in the electronics lab *and* by one of a handful of qualified techs. And that would really take some time.

But she should be able to tell whether they were damaged or not, and if not she knew how to replace them properly in their correct slots. Once they were all repaired—if necessary—and back in place...

Then, assuming the self-diagnostic showed that the servers were functioning properly, whenever the power came back on the network would reboot and communications would be restored automatically.

Of course it was dangerous to work on the relay while power was on, but she should have more than enough time to check all the circuit boards before it returned. If she got to work right away.

Chapter 11

Executive Decisions

10:10 p.m. Friday, May 27th
Near the FURC Detention Center

ANTHONY HEARD VOICES carrying through the dark as he slowly approached the security fence surrounding the shadowed hulk of the building and thought they came from outside. Which wasn't any surprise.

On his way to Security headquarters, he had recalled that all the cell doors, and every other door in the detention center, would automatically unlock if the power went out. They'd set it up that way when the place was built because they had believed only a massive cataclysm could cause the system to fail for more than a minute. It was now almost thirty since the compound had gone dark.

So Anthony had decided to go out of his way—a little detour, only—and help Michelle and Greg deal with the detainees who, as expected, had clearly left the building. Perhaps they'd taken advantage of the unlocked doors. Or maybe his officers had evacuated them.

They hadn't planned how to handle this specific situation—it wasn't one anyone had imagined would happen—but in case of fire the inmates were meant to be brought outside. So it would make sense if his officers had done that under the circumstances. On the other hand, while there were currently only two dozen or so detainees, several were real hard cases—those might not be particularly compliant. Though Michelle and Greg had both been well-trained, they might have difficulty handling things by themselves. So Anthony had headed here to help.

The security fence was merely ten feet high and without any razor wire or even barbed wire on top—he could scale that easily enough. Of course, any of the prisoners would also be able to get over it without much difficulty. If they tried to escape.

Probably some would, he thought, as a standing jump took him almost to the top of the fence. Gripping the chain links, he climbed over without clanging it too much. But moving around the compound in the dark and over broken ground would slow any escapees down. He dropped silently to the grass on the other side of the fence and headed for the nearest corner. There weren't many places for prisoners on the loose to hide, either. And they wouldn't want to go outside.

The voices grew louder, arguing, as he made his way along the side of the building. Then Michelle's sharp and clear tones cut through the babble. "Settle down, everyone, and stop milling about. Anyone who gives us any trouble will be incapacitated, then restrained, for everyone's safety."

Anthony quietly rounded the next corner to see her and Greg on the other side of a crowd of detainees. Flanking Sara King, who stood in front of them and seemed to be glaring at her fellow prisoners. It was challenging to make out any nuance in their expressions, even for him, in the deep black shadows, but people's postures spoke loudly.

His officers both had their pepper spray out and ready to use. A large white bandage covered part of Greg's head though, so obviously they'd already had some difficulty with the inmates. But not with Sara apparently. She seemed to be working with his two officers. Interesting.

The three of them seemed to have things well in hand now, so Anthony decided to hold back, to wait and watch a while, but even as he was thinking that two detainees suddenly broke away from the crowd and ran for the fence.

He sprinted across the grass, but they had both gone over the top, hit the ground, and taken off into the dark before he reached the spot. Sara King had run and leaped onto the fence by then, and Anthony jumped up to grab her and pull her back.

She turned on him in frustration. "They're getting away!"

"But you're not." Taking a firm grip on her arm and turning back toward the others, he saw his two officers had spread out to try and contain the crowd of detainees, who'd begun to disperse. "Hold!" Anthony projected his voice with authority, the way he had been trained.

And everyone, on that side of the fence at least, froze. But in that moment of quiet he heard a curse in the distance from the other side, as one of the escapees stumbled over something. Well, they would be dealt with soon enough.

Even Michelle and Greg stood like statues, looking expectantly to him. He gestured at the building. "I want the detainees to form a line in front of those doors." As the inmates began to obey, he waved his two officers closer and lowered his voice. "You saw who went over the fence?"

Michelle nodded crisply. "Brandon Radley and Jake Hennessey, sir."

Anthony bit back a curse of his own. Those two were perennial troublemakers and saboteurs who'd tried to help Governor Roberts take over the FURC, and wherever they were headed they wouldn't be up to any good. He ran his gaze over the prisoners lining up in front of the detention center and counted. "Others had already escaped?"

"No, Chief. Sara zip-tied four, and we left those inside. The rest are all accounted for."

He stared down at Sara's hard expression, then shook his head and looked back at Michelle. "You'd better give me a full report, Officer Mori." He gazed back past the security fence. "But be as brief as you can."

She took only a moment to gather her thoughts before starting. "Greg and I were in the break room when the quake hit and power went. We were wondering what to do—it hadn't occurred to either of us yet that the doors had automatically unlocked—and one of the male prisoners barged in, attacked Greg. It was Neilson, sir. Before I knew it, Sara was there taking him down. I gave her some zip-ties, then she restrained him and went to deal with other troublemakers."

A soft cough from her junior partner interrupted her, then she continued. "She'd reported a water break in the kitchen, and after I treated his injuries Greg took care of that problem. Then Sara returned to say she'd subdued and restrained three problematic prisoners and report the rest had evacuated the building. She suggested the three of us together approach those, to minimize the potential for trouble. We were just getting them calmed down when Radley and Hennessey bolted."

Anthony nodded in approval, then turned back to consider the woman whose arm he still held. She met his gaze with resignation. "Why?"

Sara shrugged. "Marigold attacked me, so I had to defend myself. Then I thought I'd better check to see if Greg and Michelle might need help. And they did. I just tried to do what was right."

And unless he missed his guess, she hadn't been trying to escape a minute ago, she'd intended to run after Brandon and Jake. Not to join them. To drag them back here by their heels if necessary. She had been a promising recruit, and it seems she retained the mentality of a security officer—in spite of all she had done.

Maybe she should be given a second chance.

He turned back to Michelle. "I saw what looked like a large meteorite strike four or five minutes before all the shaking started, so I don't think this was a typical earthquake or that there's much chance of aftershocks. And from what I've seen I doubt these buildings are in any real danger of falling down. So I want you two to drag the four who've been zip-tied into their cells, get some padlocks—you'll find them in one of the cupboards in the staff conference room

—and use those to secure them in their cells. Later, after you've taken care of everything else that needs to be done, you can cut their ties from the other side of the bars."

Officer Mori nodded. "And that everything else you mentioned, sir?"

"Just the two of you would have a difficult time managing all these inmates out here. The emergency lighting's on inside? So it should be easier to see in there anyway. I'll keep an eye on them while you and Greg put the others in their cells, then I'll want the two of you to escort the rest back inside, to their separate wards. Let them stay in their cells with the doors open."

"Sir?"

"Most won't cause you any trouble. I'll speak to them first and make sure they understand if they do they'll regret it. I'll tell them you'll padlock them in their cells too if they don't behave. And as soon as I can, I'll send a couple more officers to back you up." He sighed. "That'll have to do."

Michelle gave him another crisp nod and looked at Greg, then turned and headed for the main door. Her partner swiveled and bounded after her.

Anthony watched them enter while running his eye over the line of fidgeting prisoners. "So, Sara, I want your help to track down and recapture Radley and Hennessey." He'd rather have Kat with him for that, but she had her own job. And while all the officers they'd trained could handle a couple of criminals under normal circumstances, in this particular situation Sara was better suited to the task.

He could take care of that pair by himself, without any help, of course. But he wanted to test Sara, see what she'd do if let off the leash, find out if she'd reformed as he was starting to suspect. And having help would be useful, even if it wasn't strictly necessary. Since he had no idea what they might run into out there.

"I'm offering you a temporary parole, but if you do well..." He sighed. His job didn't include deciding an issue like this, but he'd do what was right and face down Miles and Caroline if he had to. "I'll have your sentence commuted." Perhaps even put her to work in Security again. But it was too soon to think about that, much less mention. "What do you say?"

A smile twitched at the edges of her lips. "I say I'd better not screw up this time, sir."

Chapter 12

Changing Direction

10:15 p.m. Friday, May 27th
Approaching the FURC's north gate

LT. KATHERINE MILES had started south, after grabbing her pad from their suite and seeing her husband off and heading west toward Security HQ. She'd intended to go to the Guard headquarters. It was where she worked, after all, and where she kept her sniper rifle.

But while that was normally the nerve center of operations for external security, it couldn't function as such, really, until communications were restored. Chief Cameron should be supervising things at HQ, and there would be at least a few guards there to do his bidding. What could she do? And she'd have to cross most of the compound to get there.

A huge waste of time. Especially when there'd only be two guards at the back gate, cut off and isolated. So she'd turned around and headed north.

Not only would they need reinforcements at the rear entrance, they'd require leadership. Being off-duty herself, she didn't know which of the guards on duty would be there when, but MacTierney was the sergeant in charge of this shift. He'd probably be on the main gate, unable to give orders to the guards in the buffer zone or at the back gate. He wasn't likely to be on any of those patrols himself.

Kat had rearranged things—rather than assign a pair of guards to the back gate for a whole shift, she had three pairs of guards patrolling the buffer zone and taking turns remaining at the station at that far end of the compound. When one patrol reached the back gate, they'd relieve the pair already there, who would proceed to make one full circuit of the buffer zone before relieving the third patrol. So only those on duty would know which guards should be where at any given time.

But whoever was stationed at the back gate, she worried about them. As she'd made her way in that direction as swiftly as she could in the circumstances, Kat had gotten glimpses of ever-increasing damage. Apparently that seismic wave had hit hardest to the north. Which made sense, as it must have traveled from that direction, its strength thankfully dissipating as it moved south. But that meant the pair at the north gate would've gotten the worst of it.

Moving out of the warehouse district across the Ag sector, she had seen storage sheds flattened and greenhouses shattered as if they'd imploded. Those structures had been built to less stringent specifications, of course.

Even 'Cameron's Luxury Suites' had taken more of a hit than she'd first thought—when she'd gotten to the second floor she'd found large cracks in some walls and pieces of the ceiling that had crumbled to the floor. And been grateful Steve had shut the water off so soon, else the entire building would surely have flooded. Even more thankful no one there had been seriously injured. They'd all been able to leave under their own steam, and though the place hadn't seemed about to fall down, getting everyone out had been the right call.

And now she noticed the roofs on some shelters constructed for the livestock they'd saved from outside had fallen in. The chicken coops were a bizarre mess of broken boards tangled in wire fencing, with the birds squawking in distress. Thankfully she also saw several Ag workers who must've rushed here in spite of the difficulty involved, working hard to rescue the animals.

At least there seemed enough helping that they wouldn't need her assistance. Just seeing and hearing those poor animals at such a distance made her shudder and shift her gaze away.

Still she wasn't prepared for the devastation she discerned when she finally came within sight of the back gate—cracks in the perimeter wall so large she could see them from afar in relative dark, chunks of crumbled masonry fallen to the grass below and exposing the rebar, and a shapeless mound where the guard shack had stood.

Though they called it 'the shack', the station off to one side of the gate was a tiny but well-built brick structure. One small room to take a break or write a report in, but too cramped to spend much time in.

Hopefully that meant neither of her guards had been within when the thing collapsed, but so far she couldn't see either of the pair that should have been there. At least the gate itself was closed.

That would be small consolation though, should one or both of her people be seriously injured.

Nearing the rubble she saw a shadow detach itself from what was left of the shack and resolve into a silhouette—one of the guards at least, and backing away from the remains of the station. And she soon identified that guard as Grace.

The eldest Cameron daughter had cut that long hair she used to wear in a sophisticated structure of multiple braids mercilessly short when she became a guard, got the same buzz-cut most of the men wore just before she'd transferred from Security. But she was still shorter and slighter than any of them.

Kat called out her name and was grateful to see Grace stand and start walking closer without a limp or any apparent difficulty. "You're alright. Where's your partner?"

Seeing the other woman's somber expression in the moonlight, she wasn't surprised when Grace inclined her head back toward the ruined shack. "He was slacking off. Fifty minutes into a fifteen-minute break, but Wagner was senior to me, so I didn't say anything. If I'd given him a tongue-lashing the way I should've, maybe he wouldn't have been in there."

Kat shook her head. "You can't blame yourself. And Wagner wouldn't have listened anyway." She'd continued stalking toward the rubble as they talked and could now see there was little hope the man had survived. But they couldn't assume anything. "You were trying to dig him out?"

Grace nodded. "But it's slow going." She didn't add that it was probably useless as well, but Kat saw it on her face.

"Well, with two of us it shouldn't take too long." Running her gaze along the perimeter wall again as they walked over, she could see that the worst damage was at least limited to the sections to either side of the gate. Though it made her wonder if they'd be able to open it or not. If they couldn't that would be a problem should they need to bring somebody into the compound. Which would be worse, having them try to climb over where the wall had crumbled or go seven miles or so to the main gate? Without knowing what the situation there was, Kat couldn't say.

But she knew that was a worry for later. So she and Grace focused on pulling pieces of brick off the pile, shifting chunks of wood and plastic until they'd finally uncovered what was clearly a corpse. Hardly recognizable as Wagner. But it couldn't be anybody else.

Neither needed to suggest a moment of silence, they both bowed their heads as soon as they saw the remains and folded their hands in prayer. However poor a guard he'd been, the man deserved that. And Kat's own fault for not making him better anyway—or at least firing him. Then he would not have been here to die like this.

"What do we do now, Lieutenant?" Grace stood and looked around, though it wasn't clear what for. "The patrol that relieves us wasn't supposed to show up for another hour or so, but who knows what happened to them?"

Kat settled back on her heels. "We have to stay here and guard"—she certainly couldn't leave Grace here alone to do that, even though the girl was definitely capable of handling it by herself—"what's left of the wall."

She wasn't worried about intruders or invaders at the moment—not the human variety, as anybody out there when that quake had hit surely had problems of their own to deal with, and the wall was not damaged enough to make getting over it *that* easy—they could defend this section easily enough.

But one glance had been sufficient to show that the security fence beyond was in far worse condition—with steel posts uprooted, it leaned over almost to the ground in one place, and that was just what she could see. Thankfully the buffer zone was too wide, even at its narrower points—just twenty-four feet at the corners—to turn a downed fence into a ramp up to the wall.

However, there were more and more predators of the animal variety out there. Herds of feral hogs and even the occasional bear. Panthers stalking the forest at night in ever-increasing numbers. Hungry enough to risk a collapsed fence, all of them, if they saw food walking around.

"Let's see if we can get the gate open." Bringing the guards outside into the relative safety inside the compound had to be a priority.

She walked over to the right side, where the gate slid into the frame that held it. And Grace followed with the key, which she inserted into the lock, which was set in a metal panel in the pillar that braced the end of the wall. Turning that moved gears which in turn moved others that released the clamps holding the gate in place.

Grabbing the wrought-iron bars, Kat pulled the gate back. A few inches. Barely past the pillar. She tugged harder, leaning back, and managed to move it a couple more. Enough to stick her arm through, for all the good that would do.

Grace wrapped her hands around the end of the gate and leaned in, using her body weight to push—Kat almost fell backward pulling with her—and they shifted the gate several more inches, creating clearance of a little more than a foot. Sufficient for some skinny person to squeeze through, but most guards would have a hard time.

Perhaps Kat *should* leave the other woman here to defend the wall and head out into the buffer zone to see if she could find the approaching patrol. She might not have her rifle—and the one that had been buried with Wagner wouldn't likely be of any use, if she were to retrieve it from the rubble—but she had her Glock. And she had more experience facing the wild animals out there than any of her guards.

Which was to say, she had a little while they had none.

On the other hand, men's boots could walk over the downed mesh of the security fence without a lot of difficulty, while hooves and claws might catch on the chain links. Humans could jump over the razor wire where it rested close to the ground fairly easily too, but animals might not realize they should even try. The mental images flooding her thoughts were heart breaking, and she shoved them out.

She knew some techs had been working on sonic fencing, intended to keep wild animals away once they started developing the land outside the FURC, but that was still a long way off, and she had no idea if it was ready to be deployed. But without power it didn't matter anyway.

Grace had crossed over, past the opposite pillar and up to one of the large cracks in that wall. Peering in, she sighed loudly. "The back end of the gate frame appears to be bent. I don't think we can shift it much further, and if we try we may not be able to close it again."

Kat looked at where the top of the wall had collapsed the most, exposing the rebar. Visualized her guards trying to climb over that. "Still, let's see how far we can open it."

This time she pushed it back while Grace pulled with all her body weight. It seemed to shift another inch or so before seizing with a feeling of finality, as if there was no way it would budge one more hair in either direction. And the other woman *had* warned her.

"At least if they suck in their bellies they should be able to scrape through." Scrape being the operative word. But a little laceration was better than remaining out there.

Whatever concerns she had, going out after her guards wouldn't be very smart. If the patrol coming this way was about an hour away, that meant it was around halfway from the main gate to here. And no telling if they would continue on or head back in reaction to what happened. For all she knew both patrols might be headed to the main gate. Even if she ran she might not catch up to them.

Hopefully both patrols would realize how badly they'd be needed here and be on their way. But one or more of the guards on either patrol might well be injured and waiting for help themselves.

She simply didn't know. And had always hated not knowing. Now that she was in charge, expected to give orders, and responsible for others, not knowing was simply unacceptable.

Kat took off her shoulder holster and grinned at Grace. "Hold the fort here." Moving slowly she was able to squeeze through the gap into the buffer zone without hurting herself then shrugged back into her holster. "And wish me luck."

Chapter 13
Taking Care of Business

10:20 p.m. Friday, May 27th
Approaching Community Hall

ALVIN COULD HEAR the mass milling in front of the steps up to the Hall long before he could make out the crowd standing mostly in shadow. Naturally they'd evacuated the building, but what was everyone doing just standing around talking. Who was in charge here?

Officer Wellman had set a hard pace, intuitively understanding he preferred getting on to being coddled. Or perhaps she was simply in a hurry to get to her own office. Either way, he appreciated it.

The tall skinny silhouette of Jeffrey Minchin resolved as they approached—the laconic landscaper, and fellow councilor, stood a good head higher than anyone else gathered in front of the Hall—but if the man was doing anything helpful, Alvin couldn't tell. Fox peered at the indistinct shapes as he got closer, but he couldn't find any other councilors among the crowd.

Then Susan put a hand on his arm and brought him to a halt. "If you don't mind, Mr. Fox, I'll leave you now. I think you can make it the rest of the way safely."

He nodded curtly. "Thank You, Officer." Then, continuing without looking back, wondered if she'd meant that for sarcasm. During their too brief conversation at the suite he'd rented, Alvin had started to suspect she had a deadpan sense of humor. However, it was hard to be sure. He intended to find out more about her, though. Later.

For now, he needed to focus on seeing what advantage he could discover here at the Hall. He had gotten close enough to confirm that Jeffrey was the only councilor in sight. So where was Caroline Sanderson?

"Minchin!" The man turned toward him with a blank expression. "What's going on?"

"Apparently an earthquake, Fox." Another one with a strange sense of humor.

Alvin frowned and gestured around at the other people now standing and staring. "I mean, what are you doing about it?"

Those skinny shoulders shrugged. “Waiting for the power to come back on. It’s been a while, but it shouldn’t be much longer.”

“And what gives you reason to think that?” Not a thing, Fox felt sure. An independent contractor for the FURC, Minchin might be considered a business owner by some people, but he was really just another worker with delusions of grandeur. And a fellow councilor.

At least the man ‘identified’ as a worker, though that was probably only so he could represent all the rank-and-file employees. It made him a union boss, basically, but of a different sort from what Fox was used to dealing with. Still, he wasn’t surprised that the man wasn’t doing anything. He was just as lazy as those he supposedly acted for.

Getting no answer to that question, Alvin asked another. “Where’s Caroline, then?”

“Saw Paul driving her off in a cart, earlier, to do something about the power, probably.”

‘Paul’ must be Macklin, the councilor representing the student body—though why they needed any voice on the council remained a mystery. And Minchin’s assumption about what had Caroline running off somewhere seemed to have no basis. “Are these all the people who were in the Hall, then? Someone made sure no one was left inside and injured?”

“We got everyone out, I think.”

Fox held back a sigh of exasperation. "You saw to that yourself, did you?"

Minchin blinked. "I made sure everyone in the main hall where I was evacuated. And Carmen said those in the offices got out." Glancing around, Alvin didn't see Caroline's assistant anywhere. "She and some others gathered by the back exit." He bit back an insult, knowing he had to work with the man.

They were interrupted by several voices clamoring for news, asking what he knew of what was happening in the rest of the compound and about when power would be restored. Questions concerning the well-being of people whose names he couldn't even recognize.

Addressing them as a group, he told them what little he knew. "Security officers and guards are doing what needs to be done to see everybody's safe. I talked to Lt. Miles"—dropping her name in since he knew she was popular—"and I know they're clearing buildings and searching for any injured. I also saw a couple officers on the Green, taking care of the people there, as I passed by to the north." He certainly didn't envy them, whoever they were, trying to deal with that motley lot of Friday night revelers.

He turned his attention back to his fellow councilor. "We should probably assemble everyone here in one place." As much as he wanted to, he couldn't just bark out orders. He'd have to be careful in how he handled this situation if he was going to take advantage of Caroline's absence, to increase his influence and boost his odds in the next election. "Could you walk around to the back and bring Carmen and the others here? I'd appreciate it."

After taking a long moment to stare back in apparent consideration of that reasonable request, the man finally nodded. "Sure, I can do that." Minchin took his pad out of a jacket pocket and activated the flashlight function, played its beam across the grass as he sauntered away.

Fox turned to the others milling about. "I think we should check to make sure no one was left inside the Hall, maybe injured."

No one said anything, but at least several gave a nod of agreement. "I'll go, but I'm hoping one or more of you will volunteer to accompany me." He paused for someone to speak up or raise their hand. When nobody did, he continued. "And we don't know how long it might take for them to restore power." Much less the net and their ability to communicate. "So it would be a good idea to grab some supplies while we are in there—food and first-aid kits—and I could use some help carrying stuff."

After a moment, murmurs of approval began to break the silence and a few hands went up. "OK, as soon as Councilor Minchin brings the others over to join our little group, we'll head into the Hall and see what we can find." And hopefully they'd remember that when action was called for, he was one who got things done.

And the longer Caroline was gone, the more opportunity he'd have to show them.

10:25 p.m. Friday, May 27th
On the way to Security Headquarters

SUSAN SPED ALONG the walkway as swiftly as she safely could by the light shining from her pad—stumbling over any of the cracks would only cause a further delay in getting to HQ. And ever since she'd delivered Councilor Fox to the Community Hall, she had found herself distracted by worries centered on him. Those thoughts could be as dangerous to her—to her progress—as the dark.

As satisfying as she found her work in Security, it had never been her ultimate aspiration. Knowing herself a capable officer, she wasn't surprised by the promotions, how quickly she'd gone from safety aide to officer to shift supervisor. But she'd hit a ceiling there. Chief Nelson wasn't going anywhere, and his deputy Kirkland wouldn't retire anytime soon. And she'd always had another dream, to start a business of her own and build it into a successful enterprise.

She didn't know what kind of enterprise, or how to get it off the ground in the current environment—not the aftermath of the earthquake, but with everything still mostly locked down in the compound for the foreseeable future. And Fox had given her some good ideas about that.

Of course, with his reputation, she had not been surprised when he'd suggested meeting her at Cameron's Luxury Suites—claiming he'd taken rooms to get away from the office for the weekend—and she'd known what he wanted. But she wasn't about to let him seduce her. Not that she had any objection to a potential relationship with him—in theory, at least—but whatever else he gave her, he would give her respect.

She wouldn't have to deal with that problem for a while, though. How she would face Kat was a different question—Susan considered her a friend and wanted to clear up any doubts the other woman had about what she and Fox had been doing. Somehow without making excuses, since she had no reason to be ashamed. But since Kat's mother and Councilor Fox were political rivals, it promised to be awkward between them.

Exactly what Susan had hoped to avoid by having her meeting with the man in private. She would worry about that later too, though. Seeing the dark square of Security Headquarters up ahead, she knew she should focus on what needed doing now. Someone there should, hopefully, be able to tell her what that was.

The building appeared empty from outside, but as soon as she pushed through into the lobby, those dim red emergency lights revealed Hope sitting behind the duty desk and snacking on a nutrition bar. Noticing her entrance, the young aide gave Susan a wide smile. “You know, you’re the first to show up, Officer Wellman.”

“The first?” Susan glanced behind her as if others were close on her heels. “What about Chief Nelson?” He should’ve beat her here. “I suppose Salazar and Gabe were out on patrol when it happened. With one of the carts?” Chances were, the pair had plenty of problems to deal with out there, wherever they were.

Hope nodded. “But those won’t just keep going, not for long on only their batteries. That’s what Bob says, anyway, and he should know.”

So Deputy Chief Bob Kirkland was here, apparently. He would’ve been on duty and had been here at headquarters when the quake hit from the sound of it. As had Hope, clearly. “Is anyone else around? Other officers?”

“Just Ben. He was up in the Resource Room at the time, but with the net down there isn’t anything for him to do. So he’s in the break room, refueling.”

Instead of heading out to help. Not that he ought to without a partner, and who would he take? Deputy Chief Kirkland? Hope?

"Bob's in the Chief's office?" The former sheriff liked to keep things casual. Asked everybody to call him by his first name. And just used the Chief's office when he was on duty, instead of insisting on his own. But then Nelson rarely spent time in his office anymore, so Kirkland had pretty much taken over in there.

Hope grinned. "And he'll be really happy to see you. He's been champing at the bit to get out, to do his part, but says he can't leave until a senior officer arrives to take his place. Because somebody has to coordinate our response. And until communication is restored, that means staying here to gather information and relay orders to everyone who eventually shows up."

Susan shook her head. "Why can't *you* do that? I certainly think you're capable." And better having her sit here and do that than send her out to 'help' in a crisis like this. "Bob could've taken Ben..." But that would've left Hope here on her own. And while she probably would've been safe enough, if anybody tried to take advantage and attack Security HQ, she wouldn't be able to defend this place. Or likely herself, even. "Anyway, I don't intend to sit around coordinating anything."

She pushed through the little gate beside Hope, breezed past the girl down the short corridor to the Chief's office, and knocked on the open door as she walked in. "Alright. Now I'm here, you and I can go out and see who we can help, leave Hope to 'coordinate' things and Ben to protect her." Even if he still spent most of his time staring at a pad, the boy had become a pretty capable officer, finally. Sufficiently skilled to stop a couple criminals, in case one or two troublemakers showed up here.

Kirkland chuckled. "Slow down a bit there, Susan. First, what can you tell me about the situation outside?"

"Not much. Chief Nelson was headed here, and I'm surprised he hasn't shown up yet, but I suppose he should soon. I saw Councilor Fox safely to Community Hall. Saw a small crowd of people who had evacuated the building, but they didn't look to need any real help. Just waiting around for somebody to tell them what to do." And Alvin would surely take care of that. "I covered a good bit of ground getting here, and from what I could see things aren't so bad out there."

The big man leaned back in his chair and shook his head. "That's not surprising. I mean, we hardly get anything worth calling a quake in Florida, so it's to be expected when we do get one that it's not a big deal." He leaned forward again. "But there will still be problems out there that need to be handled, even if it's just calming people down. And keeping them quiet until the power's back and life starts returning to normal."

"Sounds about right, sir." She paused. "But we won't really know until we see for ourselves."

Kirkland nodded. "I'd thought I'd take Ben out on patrol once somebody like you showed up, but if Nelson's on his way it should be okay to leave Hope and him here on their own." He grinned. "And the Chief can be the one to sit behind this desk and 'co-ordinate' everything."

Susan felt sure the man would object if he were here, but he wasn't. "Then let's get moving. Before he shows up. I'll inform Ben and Hope of our plan, then meet you at the carts." A couple of the buggies should be parked by the side of the building. Stalking out of the office, she headed for the break room. Time for Ben to stop eating and earn his pay.

10:30 p.m. Friday, May 27th
Southwest section of the buffer zone

TIM RELIED ON the moonlight to show him any significant damage to the security fence or wall, because he didn't want to waste the battery on his pad and doubted its light would reveal minor damage—small cracks or split chain links. Also, he wanted to make the best time he safely could. That meant not inspecting too carefully as he trotted past, whatever Chief Cameron had said. It hadn't been an order as such.

At least the Chief had agreed that someone senior should be sent to the back gate and allowed Tim to assign himself that job. MacTierney had decided to take the west side of the buffer zone because that way he would be the one to meet the guards headed toward the main gate, and only he of those available had the authority to order them to turn around and go back to the north gate. Though orders relayed by any of the others should've sufficed. Tim needed to be sure.

He had sent Patience around the east side even though the youngest Cameron girl had only recently joined the Guards—had just a month ago turned old enough to be allowed to—because she could run like the wind. Not that he wanted her to sprint—he had specifically told her to be careful and take her time—but she would still travel faster than anyone else he could have sent. And she tended to be rather hasty, belying her name, so she might speed along anyway despite his orders. Which could land her in hot water with her father, if he found out. But MacTierney had covered his own rear end.

Her job was merely to catch up to the other patrol, the one which should already be headed to the back gate to relieve Grace and Wagner. To get them to hurry there and reinforce that pair.

He'd also told her to observe and note the damage to the security fence and perimeter wall on that side of the compound, the same as he was supposed to be doing. He'd seen some bent posts and fencing that had bowed outward and a single sizeable crack in the wall and recorded the general position on his pad—and doubted she was doing any better job of it than he. Hopefully she wasn't doing much worse.

Up ahead to the left he noticed a fence post that had seemingly launched straight up out of the earth and now hung in the air slightly above ground, supported only by the chain links stretching between it and the posts on either side. That left a little gap at the bottom where someone, or something, would be able to squeeze through if they tried. Wouldn't take much to pull the post down, push the base back into its hole so it at least looked secure. But he only took out his pad and made a note so someone could fix it later. *He* had to reach Grace as soon as possible.

About half an hour had passed, according to his pad, since he'd set out from the main gate. So if the other patrol had continued on, he should meet them before long. Another hour and a half—if they didn't run into trouble—to get to the back gate. Too long.

Trotting along, he heard a kind of grunt behind him a few minutes later and stopped, turned to see a feral hog in the buffer zone, charging toward him.

Even as he dropped to a knee, bringing the rifle —which the chief had insisted he take with him—to his shoulder, he wondered if the creature had come through the gap he'd recently passed. Didn't matter now, though.

By the time he was sighting the target, that hog was too close for even him to miss. But as much as he hated those things, he didn't want it to suffer, so he took an extra moment to aim as best he could.

Despite his racing heart, MacTierney forced his breathing to slow down, drawing out each breath so it hardly seemed he was breathing at all, just like Lt. Miles had taught him. Steadied his muscles, turned perfectly still. Then gently moved only his finger on the trigger.

The loud crack of the shot and the recoil kicking his shoulder back knocked him on his butt. Rolling backward and onto his feet, his breathing came quick and labored now, but he didn't care. He strode forward up to the fallen creature and saw the hole he'd made. In the hog's forehead, right between the eyes —it was dead, of course, and it had been quick. And as painless as possible.

MacTierney sighed and stalked back toward the gap in the fence. At least he ought to be able to prevent any more of the animals from finding their way into the buffer zone through that. Whether this one had gotten in that way or not.

Getting a good grip on the chain links with both hands, one to either side of the wayward post, MacTierney struggled to pull it down. Lining the bottom end of the post up with the black hole in the shadowed grass made it even more awkward. A lot more difficult than he'd thought.

Then a sudden cry came, and another loud rifle crack came a split second later, followed by a familiar voice shouting. "Head right back out unless you want the next one in the head."

MacTierney cursed under his breath. And gave thanks they were taught to fire warning shots. "Put your gun away, Alvarez! Unless you want an official reprimand in your file." He sighed. "Now, come on and help me with this thing."

Together they managed to drag the fence down and wrestle the post back into the ground, push it in far enough it seemed to hold. It wouldn't take much to pull it up again and create a gap to slip in, but no one should know that. So as long as it appeared secure...

As soon as they'd finished, Tim blew out a huge breath and turned to Alvarez. "Where's Hodges?"

The other man shook his head. "I guess he never learned how to fall. Fool seems to have sprained his ankle. At least, I hope it's not broken. But he is whining so much it's hard to tell." He laughed. "So I left him where he was sitting and massaging himself when I heard your shot." He had certainly seen the dead hog, and whistled when they walked past. "Well done, by the way."

MacTierney ignored that. "I was ordered to get you and Hodges turned around, to reinforce the two at the north gate, but you'll have to help Hodges get back to HQ instead." He'd just have to continue on his own. Try to make better time. Because as far as he knew, Grace might not have any.

Chapter 14

Working Overtime

10:35 p.m. Friday, May 27th
Living room of the Courdray residence

OFFICER LISA COURDRAY shoved frantically at the debris trapping her in darkness. She had difficulty breathing and knew she had to get free soon, to break the surface and find air to fill her lungs. As she struggled, the screaming claxon kept drumming in her ears. She couldn't remember what the alarm meant, specifically—only that it heralded imminent disaster.

An incomplete jumble of fragmented memories crowded her thoughts. Walls collapsing and pieces of the ceiling crashing down on her, like shards of a nightmare. The roaring of an approaching train, or a tornado. Fire unseen and wind unfelt around her everywhere like a burning fog, and all the while the alarm increasing in intensity, pounding in her skull at the back of her eyes.

She pushed and pushed, and suddenly her eyelids popped open to reveal a pitch-black night. The alarm going off was a lot quieter now—it came from her pad as it flashed like a beacon in the darkness—and she shut it off with her thumb without thought. Why had she set the alarm? Why should she feel as if she had swum up from the depths of the ocean?

As the remnants of the nightmare faded, something of real memory returned. A long day working for Security, then picking Joey up from the care center and dropping him off at the house where a friend was having a birthday party. There had been plenty of parents there to chaperone, so she had taken advantage of the rare opportunity to return home and spend some time alone. Set the alarm for when she needed to head back and pick up her kid before hitting the wine. Relaxed on the couch and unwinding fast, she must've fallen asleep there.

Joey. How deep under had she been? And how long had that alarm been going off before it eventually pulled her out of her slumber?

She tapped the pad in her hand, saw the time in the bottom corner of the screen, and realized it was already far past when she should've picked him up. Opening her contact list, she found Brooke Barrington, the friend's mother, so she could let the woman know she was on her way—would be soon enough—but the call wouldn't connect. Then she saw the net was down.

Sitting up straight, Lisa brushed some pieces of plaster off her chest without thought, then her eyes darted to the ceiling. She couldn't see anything and the lights wouldn't come up.

Power was out as well as the net, and part of the ceiling had fallen on her—something had given rise to those horrible images in her nightmare, and now she knew there'd been a real disaster. Of some sort. She didn't know what, or where her son was. What she did understand was that she needed to find him right away and make sure he was alright.

Standing on shaky legs, she activated the flashlight function on her pad. Ignoring the mess caused by the wineglass falling from her hand—she must've zonked out suddenly—she played the beam over the carpet and crossed carefully to the foyer. Along the way she distantly noted a number of books that had flown from their shelves to the floor, an overturned chair, and the large viewing pad lying askew next to the baseboard against the wall it had fallen from.

But cleaning up could wait, her son couldn't.

Opening the door, she stumbled outside, where at least there was light from the gibbous moon and a smattering of stars. She tried to orient, but found it unaccountably difficult. Couldn't remember exactly where the house was, where Joey's friend lived, despite having just left him there a few hours ago, and had only a vague idea how to get there. What a rotten mother she was turning out to be.

If the net were up she could get directions—and the lights pacing the walkways would be on, and she could call the woman and make sure Joey was okay and stop worrying. So she made her way as quickly as she could by the light from her pad while praying the power returned soon. Thankfully where she had to go was only several blocks away. Far enough her head had a chance to clear.

It seemed a lot farther as she needed to stop occasionally and reorient, got a little lost once or twice as she struggled to recall what the house looked like as well as the ones on either side. Finally she found it, dark and quiet. Which didn't help her feel better at all.

Striding up to the front door, she knocked a little loudly, but this was far from a normal visit. And she wasn't feeling particularly polite.

She breathed a sigh of relief as the door opened seconds after the echo of her pounding had faded to reveal the strained face of Brooke. The other mother had her own five-year old boy clutched close.

"Officer Courdray." The woman's voice sounded a little tight. Whether because of the situation or the hour or Lisa's job wasn't clear. And didn't matter at the moment.

"Where's Joey?"

The woman's satisfied smile seemed grim. "You should have stayed."

Lisa sighed. They'd said they didn't need her to stick around and help supervise, but she had known it was because they didn't like her disciplining their kids. Didn't seem to care to discipline their children at all, from what she'd seen, and she had shared her opinion rather freely. She'd never been part of this circle of stay-at-home moms and supposed she never would be. But if they weren't exactly friends, she was still surprised by their attitudes sometimes. As she was now. "Joey?" Surely the woman would not take her dislike of Lisa out on the boy.

"He's gone." Brooke paused and examined Lisa for a moment. "After the quake hit—and everybody was alright, we made sure of that—the other fathers and mothers wanted to take their kids home immediately. I would've been willing to keep yours here, however long it took you to show up and claim him. But Mrs. Rose offered to take him home, since your house is on the way to hers."

Lisa closed her eyes and repressed a sigh. "And where does Mrs. Rose live?" The woman had failed to bring Joey home. "I'd appreciate directions." As far as Lisa had seen, the disaster—an earthquake?—

hadn't done that much damage, but it was still possible they'd had some sort of accident along the way. Only, she hadn't seen anything like that as she came here.

She got a sharp look from Brooke, and what she hoped were good directions to the Rose residence—gave the other mother a tight smile and curt thanks in return. Whirling, she stalked across the grass on a rising tide of rage. If that woman had only kept her Joey as she'd said she would, Lisa would already be reunited with her boy. If Mrs. Rose had brought him home, even better.

But now she had no idea where her kid actually was, only a slim lead to follow. She'd go to the Roses'—though she wasn't sure she should hope to find the woman there or not—and if she didn't find Joey there, hopefully there would be someone who could tell her where he was. If not, she'd scour the neighborhood for him, then the rest of the compound. If that was what it took.

She paid more attention to her surroundings as she returned along roughly the route she'd taken to Brooke's, saw a few people cautiously coming out of their houses to look for damage. But no one injured or in distress, and no Mrs. Rose or any little kids.

Being more aware was why she saw him, though—the skinny fellow furtively darting from the shadow of one house to another—and knew he was up to no good. She'd been a cop too long, even before becoming a security officer here, not to have acquired an instinct. A nose for troublemakers.

She changed course toward him, trying to move as quietly as possible. But with the natural sense of prey for the hunter, he stopped and turned his head in her direction, then took off in the opposite. Naturally she gave chase.

He wasn't running for his life, however, and she was fueled with the burning desire to find her Joey, and she used that to give her speed. And luckily she didn't trip over the uneven ground.

Before she knew it, Lisa was almost on him. He whirled and threw a wild haymaker which she easily ducked, driving her head into his midriff—doubling him over—then snapped the top of her head up into his descending jaw. When he came back, incredibly with another swing at her, she spun in tight to slam the back of her fist into his temple, sending the man straight to the ground in a heap. As if somebody had suddenly cut the strings holding him up.

Shining the light from her pad on him, she recognized the traitor Jake Hennessey—who should've been locked up in the detention center. Except, the power going out would've automatically opened the cells and unlocked all the doors.

Too bad she didn't have any zip-ties on her, but if she couldn't restrain him at least she knew he was not going to be getting up again anytime soon. She started to walk away, back toward the Roses', when a voice called out. "Hey! What's going on? Who're you? And what the blazes did you do to that guy?" A large, muscular man about fifty yards off was heading toward her, and she tensed. Wondered what he might do and prepared mentally for another fight.

"Security Officer Lisa Courdray. This guy was a prisoner who escaped. Who are you?"

The approaching man had slowed as she spoke, and she couldn't see his expression, but she heard a smile in his voice when he answered. "Lt. Miles has mentioned you. I'm Guard Sergeant Steve Rose and I think our boys know each other. Your kid—what's his name?"

Good to see he was being careful. "Joey. And I am certainly glad I ran into you." Though it was the other way around. "I need to restrain this guy, but I don't have any zip-ties on me. Off the clock but not off duty." Never that.

He nodded. "My house isn't far, I could run and get some rope to tie his hands with."

"Help me drag this sorry specimen there and tie him up. I was headed to your house anyway."

Rose had reached her by then and frowned, not liking the idea of bringing a criminal home she supposed. But he took one of the guy's arms while she took the other, and together they began hauling him across the grass. "Say, Officer Courdray, any chance I can get credit for whatever time I take helping you deal with this guy?"

Lisa laughed. "Not much. But I'll log it in once the net's back up, and cross my fingers."

"Just don't forget to knock on wood. And make sure my name gets in your report." He grinned and fixed his gaze on the way forward. "You were on the way to my house? Why?"

She sighed. "Looking for my boy. And thinking your wife may know where he is."

He frowned again and said no more until they'd arrived at his front door. She propped her prisoner up against the stoop while Steve knocked then went inside. A minute later he came out, with a length of rope in his hand and Mrs. Rose following, pulling a sobbing Joey after her.

But Lisa's little boy's face lit up when he saw his mother. "Mom! Where've you been?"

"Searching for you, silly." She lifted her eyes to meet Mrs. Rose's gaze. "Brooke said you had taken him home. I'd assumed that meant *my* home."

The plump, middle-aged woman nodded. "I did stop by your place and pounded on the door but got no response. I figured you were out, and that you'd eventually make your way here."

Lisa vaguely recalled a horrible pounding noise in the middle of her nightmare. She'd assumed until now that had been related to the quake, but apparently not. "I'm glad I did." She grabbed her kid and held him close. "Should've been sooner, but I finally got you, kiddo."

Mrs. Rose beamed happily. Her husband stared at the unconscious fugitive on the lawn, leaning his shoulder against the stoop. "What about him?"

"I'll tie his hands, and the rope to the rail. But I can't take him anywhere, so you'll just have to keep him there until we can call it in and have somebody from Security come collect him. And return him to the detention center where he belongs."

He clearly didn't care for the idea, but must not have had a better one since he didn't respond. Mrs. Rose, however, had a wonderful idea. "Rather than head back to an empty house, why not stick around here with us until power returns? You and Joey are more than welcome. And this is a good night not to be alone."

Lisa looked down at her son's face and saw that he approved. "Alright. Thank you..."

"Colleen. And let Steve tie up your prisoner."

She followed Colleen into the house holding her Joey and feeling a huge sense of relief.

Chapter 15

Unwanted Jobs

10:40 p.m. Friday, May 27th
In the middle of the Green

SALAZAR GAVE HIS partner a subtle nod, permission to play bad cop. Gabe topped him by a few inches, and she was more muscular too—something he'd resented at first, along with her being a former meter maid. Or parking enforcement officer, whatever politically correct term the brass had last ruled must be used. Michael Salazar had left the force because of the way things were changing, went private a long time back and never regretted it—and he felt modern policing had only gone downhill since.

He'd only taken the job at the FURC because of the pay, and because Nelson had promised it would be different. It had certainly been that.

Then the former Feeb had saddled him with the partner he had now. Gabrielle—who everyone called Gabe—looked like an Amazon, tall and wide, with a face that would more aptly be called handsome than beautiful. And Salazar had expected her to be butch and a stickler for the rules, always arguing with him and trying to bust his balls. He'd been wrong.

At the moment she loomed quite effectively at a pair of Ag workers who'd been insisting they had to go to work—as if anyone could do much of anything without power. They certainly hadn't gotten orders from anyone to report to the Ag Center.

Not with the net still down. As he was patiently explaining to them as Gabe glared and scowled.

The two men backed down pretty swiftly, denying Salazar the opportunity to be 'even worse cop' to her 'bad cop'. Which, with her, truly was an act. He had learned quite quickly that for all her intimidating appearance, the woman was actually really nice and sweet, even. A gentle soul who enjoyed playing the part of the heavy.

They worked well together and had stayed partners all this time while the other officers seemed to switch around like they were playing musical chairs —a reference he didn't share with Gabe, to avoid reminding her how old he was. As the hills.

Casting a gimlet eye over the massive crowd, he almost wished they'd been patrolling anywhere else but the Green, because this motley lot had proved to be a handful. Of course, that was the very reason he and Gabe had been there.

Friday and Saturday nights always meant plenty of people coming to enjoy themselves in a variety of ways in the free, open space. A park in the shape of a circle, two hundred fifty yards across. Concrete walkways like spokes on a wheel cut the vast stretch of lawn into wedges like a pie. He always had loved mixed metaphors. And he understood why a courting couple might enjoy picnicking under the stars—if it weren't for the other people who came to party. Unruly groups, mostly, blasting music and shouting at each other. And sometimes coming to blows. So whoever was on patrol tended to spend a lot of time at or near the Green, in case they were needed.

And this evening he and Gabe had been driving by when the quake hit. Tossed the pair of them out of their cart, sprayed broken tree branches all over, and caused pandemonium among the civilians. Getting everyone calmed down—some were scared and some were agitated and infuriated at being told they had to settle down—had been hard enough. Getting control of the situation was something they continued to work on.

So many people—nervous and needing to know what was going on, what had happened to family or friends who weren't there, and no way for anyone to find out—and some of them injured. Not many and not seriously, but Salazar had been glad to have the medical kit on the cart. And thrilled to discover the doctor and his nurse wife among the picnickers and willing to help. Once pressed.

After treating minor scrapes and bruises caused by people being tossed around by the initial shock—there wasn't much around here hard enough to hurt anyone banging into it—the pair of medicos had begun treating the more serious injuries suffered during the fistfights that had broken out. Mayhem, but not as bad as before the Lift Virus, when the Gravity Bug inflamed the masses even more. Because after all, people were still people. And now Salazar spied that doctor heading his way, to complain again. To make more demands.

A little over six feet with thick sandy brown hair and an imperious attitude, the man glowered at the pair of officers. "You need to let us leave. I've done what I can here"—he snorted, to remind them what he thought of their insistence he and his wife should treat the injured—"and I'm sure they need me at the Medical Center. Urgently."

Salazar sighed. "Without power, how is anyone going to get somebody in dire need of surgery to the clinic?" The first time the man had approached him and Gabe, he'd shoved his pad—showing his identification as a FURC surgeon—in their faces, then demanded they take him to the Medical Center immediately. And his wife, though including her seemed more of an afterthought. But even if they'd been inclined to do so, the cart's battery wouldn't get them halfway there.

The man sneered. "The clinic does have ambulances, you know, that run on gas." He hadn't liked their 'excuse' for not driving him there.

"And with communications out, how would the med techs know someone needed them or where to go? No, there's not much point to you leaving until power is restored, and then I'll be happy to take you to the Medical Center." Happy to get rid of the guy, but it amounted to the same thing. "Until then, you can make yourself useful here."

Salazar shared a look with Gabe—not long until they'd normally be going off duty, but under the circumstances they wouldn't be. Not for hours yet.

10:45 p.m. Friday, May 27th
The FURC Medical Center Operating Theater

AMITA'S HANDS SHOOK as she scrubbed up, and she hoped none of the sisters noticed. She had done a surgery rotation back in med school, but she wasn't qualified much less up to something like this

—actual, literal brain surgery. There wasn't anyone else, though.

Neither of the staff surgeons had shown up yet, so Amita—who had only occasionally treated actual patients over the last twenty years, she was mostly a researcher—Amita had to perform a dangerous and delicate operation. Otherwise the patient would die. Definitely die, whereas there was only a four in five chance she would kill him. This was like working in third-world conditions.

Before everything fell apart, a trauma victim requiring emergency surgery would have been medevacked to the nearest properly equipped and staffed facility, where a team of specialized surgeons would spend hours operating on a patient if needed. That time was long past.

Everyone at the FURC had to rely on what could be done here, by the staff at the Medical Center and with the equipment and supplies they had on hand. Not that this was a third-world facility. Some fairly advanced equipment here, and world-class medical minds—if she did say so herself. But neither the assortment nor amount of supplies that a trauma center would require. One of their doctors, the internist, only happened to be a qualified surgeon because the director always *tried* to hire the best. The other was a top-flight orthopedic surgeon, true. But Laurie hadn't worked for the clinic until the compound had been cut off from the outside, and then only after he'd been pressured to help. Still, if one of them were here, even him...

At least a number of experienced med techs and nurses—for whom Amita was deeply grateful—were on hand to help her.

Finished scrubbing up, she turned to the surgical sister and nodded as another dried her hands on a sterile towel. This wouldn't be her first operation today. Just a few minutes ago she'd finished fixing a torn peritoneum and splicing somebody's intestine. A simple procedure compared to what she was preparing to attempt.

She followed the sisters into the operating room praying for a second success. Already one man had died, a guy with multiple fractures in both legs who David had brought in earlier. With a number of cut vessels, he'd already bled too much internally by the time they got him here—too much to survive even if both the real surgeons had been here. He'd supposedly jumped out a second-story window, but being a dunce didn't mean he should die. Only, sometimes there wasn't anything anyone could do.

Looking down at the patient prepped on the table, she hoped that wouldn't be the case with him—the man was a new resident David had just brought in for examination that evening and hadn't yet been given the Lift Virus. So he wouldn't have developed the improved immune system enjoyed by older residents. Thankfully they had built up a store of plasma donated by them for this very purpose.

Not *this* exactly—the nurses had already shaved the middle-aged man's head, inserted a central line in his neck, and draped him in one of the disposable sterile paper sheets. But many of the refugees coming into the compound were in pretty bad shape and couldn't survive the Lift Virus without help. Plasma containing the super lymphocytes got them through 'the flu' until it triggered the transformation of their own immune systems. She hoped they had enough to get them through this crisis.

Amita sighed behind her mask, happy she'd had her eyes lasered and no longer wore glasses to have fog up on her, and focused on the task at hand. The patient had been given general anesthetic by one of the med techs and was completely under. His vital signs were stable, and she should begin.

She'd noticed when they first found him that he had a depressed skull fracture. And scans had subsequently revealed broken bits of bone pressing into his brain and causing a subarachnoid hemorrhage—there really was no time to waste. Maneuvering the mechanical arm suspended from the ceiling, to line up the laser scalpel with the marks already made on his forehead by the surgical nurse, she began slicing off his scalp.

Once that had been peeled back, Amita began to gently remove small pieces of his skull—sometimes having to use the scalpel to finish detaching a chunk of bone that still clung to the skull cap—which then exposed the bleeding beneath. “Suction.”

One of the sisters repeatedly siphoned off blood every time she called out, and once she had created a clean hole it was easier to see the cut vessels. Too tiny to do anything but cauterize. Using the magnified view on the screen on the side of the machine’s ‘hand’, she locked the coordinates into its computer —grateful it didn’t rely on the net to work. And then programmed in the sequence of firings.

Taking a deep breath, she had the sisters check that his head was completely immobilized, then she double-checked the laser scalpel settings herself. A touch of a button then set the program in motion.

As soon as it had finished, she called for suction again and examined the area with the magnifier until she was sure there was no more bleeding. Then a sister held out a tray and Amita took the composite patch—much better than a metal plate—and placed it over the hole in the man’s skull. Special glue was used to affix it to the bone.

She let the surgical nurse replace the scalp over the skull and use regular sutures to join the skin—it would make the man look like Frankenstein’s monster until his hair grew back. Leaving the rest to the sisters and med techs, Amita turned away and took off her mask as she strode out of the operating room and plopped down in one of the plastic chairs.

Resting her head in her hands, she prayed again for the patient. Prayed they'd have power restored, hopefully before the generator ran out of gas. Asked God to get the real surgeons there before she had to operate on anyone else. And hoped the worst of the disaster was past.

Then she wondered where David was, when she would see him again, and whether this had changed anything between them.

Chapter 16

Full Circle

10:50 p.m. Friday, May 27th
Approaching Guard Headquarters

DAVID FINALLY REACHED the Guard HQ to find the place standing dark. With no lights shining out the windows or through the glass doors—a dim, red glow from the emergency lights was almost undiscernible from outside—the building seemed empty. But at least, at last, he'd arrived.

The real distance between the clinic and Guard headquarters wasn't that great, but even after helping carry that injured idiot to the medical center, he had found himself answering other calls for help as he tried to make his way here. No one needing help getting to the clinic, thankfully, but someone whose house was slowly flooding because they didn't know how to turn off the water. And a couple more needing minor first-aid and asking David to do whatever he could for them as he passed by. Of course he had to go slow to avoid tripping—injuring himself would do no one any good. And that gave people plenty of opportunity to seek his help.

Pushing through one of the wide doors into the lobby, he saw two guards standing with rifles ready and lifting as he entered. "Stand down, it's me—Sgt. Belue, in case you can't see my face." The men recognized his voice and swiftly lowered their weapons and saluted.

He also saw a strange little group sitting on the hard plastic chairs against the south wall. A mature woman with her arm in a sling and three children—the oldest was a girl of ten, or twelve or thirteen for all David could say, and the youngest a four- or five-year-old boy—all sporting bandages and looking extremely weary. People who had come seeking safety inside the compound, and come at a bad time.

"The Chief in his office?" Breezing past the pair of guards without waiting for their answer, he raced down the hall and barged into the outer office. Sgt. Carruthers stood inside, next to the secretary's desk —which was otherwise abandoned at the moment—with a vacant look in his eyes. David heard a string of soft curses coming from Ken's inner office. Tried to get the other sergeant's attention. "Malcolm?"

Hearing his name lured Sgt. Carruthers back to the here and now. "Belue. There are some new refugees out in the lobby. They're yours now."

"I saw. You were in the barracks, I take it, when the quake hit?" Malcolm was on the midnight shift, and the man might've even been asleep. "Since you got here pretty quick."

The older black man nodded. "One other guard there at the time, he's in the lobby now with the on-duty man. All other personnel are at the gates or in the buffer zone. The fence is down in parts, and the main gate won't close. Everyone is needed to make sure no one takes advantage, but I'm stuck here."

David sighed. But it sounded like they were on top of the situation. "And the other off-duty guards are where?"

The sergeant shrugged. "Out on the Green, over at the Rec center? With the net down, who knows? I suppose they'll eventually make their way here."

Suppressing another sigh, David strode past the other man. "I suppose you want me to escort those newcomers to the clinic, Chief? They're pretty busy over there, but—" He cut off as he reached the open doorway and saw a gray-faced Ken Cameron sitting back in his chair with his leg swathed in gauze, stiff as a board and slanted across the top of the desk. His secretary stood over him with a determined expression.

Which she then turned on David. "Will you talk some sense into him? A broken leg means he needs to go to the clinic, not sit around here bellowing orders, especially when everything's under control, or as much as can be under the circumstances."

Ken glared at her, then transferred his scowl to him. "Circumstances change. If I leave orders to be passed on while I'm gone, what happens when they need to be altered and I'm not here to do it?"

David shook his head. "Next you'll say it's only a sprain and no big deal. But she's right. You need to go to the medical center and get that leg seen to." He glanced back at Malcolm, who'd come up behind him. "Carruthers here has the experience to change the orders if the situation warrants. And as soon as power is restored—which shouldn't be too long—the net will be back up. Then you can get in touch with everyone through your pad." Unless the sisters had been forced to sedate him, but he wouldn't mention that possibility.

"I'd feel better leaving you in charge here, inexperienced as you are."

"He knows what to do better than I, as you well know, Chief."

Cameron huffed. "If only Lt. Miles were here, I could leave the Guards in safe hands."

David heaved a loud sigh. "And she's surely on her way. What do you think *she'll* say if she arrives to find you're still here refusing to get that leg treated?" If anyone could intimidate Ken into anything, she would. But David didn't like the idea of leaving his old friend waiting for however long it took her to get here. "Look, I've got to take those newcomers to the med center anyway, and I'm not sure they could walk there." He turned to Carruthers. "Is the large cart parked in the side lot?"

"Should be." The sergeant nodded. Then shook his head. "But without power, will the battery have enough juice to take you all the way to the clinic?"

Those large carts—also used for pulling the tram cars—had more powerful engines and consequently bigger batteries. "I'm sure it will." With only those five passengers and no cars to pull, it should. Especially if he left the lights off. He'd just traveled that same route here, and there was enough illumination from the moon and stars to see the walkway, even in the dark. "The problem now is getting him safely to the cart." He'd take Ken's current silence for acquiescence and try to keep things moving too fast to allow any argument.

Carruthers almost smiled. "You know the seats for those long benches on the sides of the carts, they can be detached. We could use one like a stretcher. If it'll hold his weight." He only glanced at the glaring Chief. "I think the two of us can carry him from here to there."

David wasn't so sure, but unable to think of any better plan he nodded and turned to Ken's secretary with a request. "Could you tell one of the guards in the lobby"—he realized he'd better bring whoever it was along for the ride—"whichever one looks like he weighs less, tell him to escort the newcomers to the cart in the side lot. And then to the clinic. I'll need help carrying the chief inside once I get there."

She looked at Ken. "Think you can manage for a few minutes without me?"

Cameron grumbled wordlessly in response—the man must be in bad shape—and she turned to shoo David and Malcolm out of the office ahead of her.

Out in the small parking area exclusively for HQ personnel sat the large cart capable of carrying over a dozen guards comfortably. Or at least without being squeezed *too* tight.

David used the flashlight function on his pad so Malcolm could see to disengage the clamps holding one of the long bench seats, with its thin padding, in place. And watched carefully so he could repeat the procedure when he reached the clinic. Or got however close the cart's battery could get them.

Carrying the barely padded plank easily enough on his own, Carruthers marched right back into the building with David sprinting ahead of him to open the door. The secretary had already returned to the office and held Ken's hand while they laid the board down on the desk, then slowly and carefully shifted him out of his chair to lie on the thin cushion. "Too bad we don't have a pillow for your head," David said as a joke.

But the secretary nodded as if at a suggestion—she opened one of the larger desk drawers and took out a small pillow. "You won't say one word to anyone about this." And she gently lifted Ken's head to slide the pillow under it.

Thankfully the chief seemed to be drifting off as David and Malcolm each grabbed one end of the improvised stretcher. Awkwardly backing out with his end, David carried it out of the office and anteroom and set the pace as the pair made their way through the short corridor and back out into the parking lot. Ortiz was already there, standing over the four asylum seekers who sat on the bench on the other side, the one that still had its seat.

The two sergeants set the seat with Ken on it in place. Carruthers clicked the clamps down as David slid into the driver's seat in front, then glanced back over his shoulder at the skinny guard the chief's secretary had chosen. "Ortiz, reach across the divider. Make sure he doesn't slide off while we're moving." David grinned at Malcolm. "Guess you're in charge, Carruthers."

"Until Lt. Miles makes it here. Or communications are restored, whichever comes first." Malcolm gave him a grim smile. "You just make sure to take good care of the chief."

David nodded. "Will do." As the other sergeant turned and marched back into the building, he took a moment to breathe slow and consider his route to the clinic. Every extra yard he traveled depleted the battery, so it was important not to detour any more than safety required.

Also, acceleration used up more energy, so slow and steady would best preserve the battery level. It wasn't like there was a need for speed, either. So he hoped.

Turning the wheel so he could maneuver out of the lot without backing up, he turned the key in the ignition and gently pushed his foot on the 'gas'. The cart hummed and rolled across the blacktop over to the accessibility ramp onto the cement walkway behind the building.

That ramp had originally been built for those in wheelchairs or on scooters, but nobody in the compound needed such things for mobility. Hadn't for a long time anyway, thanks to the changes the Lift Virus had initiated. But he had a hard time imagining Ken—or that guy who'd shattered both legs—getting around without such devices. At least he'd noticed a few sitting around in storerooms at the med center, so they'd be available. He hoped there wouldn't be a lot of people needing them.

The walkways curved quite a bit as they wound their way through the compound, but they were still fairly direct paths from one point to another, and he doubted going off onto the grass, across in a slightly straighter line, and back onto the walkway would be shorter enough to be worth the risk. Moonshadows meant he had to peer carefully at the cement rolling toward the cart as it advanced, but at least he could see. The vast swaths of lawn between the buildings were almost black in the night. Without headlights on to disperse the dark.

So he kept the cart trundling along the walkway that went past the clinic, easing off when approaching any of the larger cracks in the cement and accelerating after he'd gotten over them. Each time as it bumped he'd glance quickly back to make sure Ken wasn't about to slide off. But always saw Ortiz with one hand holding hard to the chief's shirt.

The middle-aged woman gripped a bar with one hand and held her other arm tightly around the two youngest children. Probably they were hers, but he had learned to avoid assumptions like that.

And before he knew it they were getting close to the clinic. Slowing down to take the turn, the cart's whine faltered, but he managed to get it halfway up the broad stretch paving the way to the main doors before the engine cut out, then coast another couple feet before friction canceled their momentum.

Sending the family of four ahead of them, David detached the bench seat Ken was lying on. Then he and Ortiz took opposite ends and carried him on in through the doors the woman's daughter was holding open for them. Across the lobby, through more doors, and into the emergency room.

There he found a weary, bleary-eyed Amita taking a look at the gash in someone's head. Not really her job, but they were far busier than when he'd left the last time and still short on staff from the look of things. She saw him and came over as a couple med techs were helping him and Ortiz transfer Ken from the makeshift stretcher to one of the beds.

His old friend was mostly unconscious now and moaning softly. "I hope you can fix him up fast."

Amita was running a scanner over the bandaged leg. "*I* hope our orthopedic surgeon decides to show up soon."

Chapter 17

Resolve

11:15 p.m. Friday, May 27th
FURC Director's Office, Administration Building

CAROLINE SLOWLY LIFTED her head so she could gaze down at her husband's face—in the hazy red glow and with his eyes closed, Miles managed to look peaceful. At rest. And she supposed he would be, now.

Lying her left cheek back on his chest, she wondered why she hadn't been taken with him, why she had been left behind to face everything on her own. There was Kat, of course, and her relationship with her daughter had certainly improved a lot. But they didn't spend much time in each other's company.

She sighed, and a couple more tears leaked out, but she'd pretty much cried herself empty. Nothing to do now but stay here with him and wait for whoever came. For him, for her, it didn't matter.

Bright, white light suddenly filled the room, and her head jerked up again. She looked around in expectation, but she remained alone. It had only been the power coming back on, though that was at least *something* positive, to lift the gloom a little.

Looking back down, she no longer saw her husband. Instead of Miles, peacefully resting almost as if sleeping, what lay on the carpet was just a lifeless shell, a revoltingly hollow husk. Caroline stood and stepped away before catching herself.

While it wasn't her husband anymore, the thing should be shown some respect. Glancing about, she wondered what to do with the corpse. Leaving it lying there on the floor seemed wrong somehow—but when she squatted down to grab the shoulders, with the idea of dragging it over to and up onto the couch against the wall, she found it far too heavy for her.

At least she had closed his eyes so they stopped staring into infinity. Fetching a blanket from one of the drawers in the end table next to the sofa, though not the pillow which he wouldn't need anymore, she draped it over his body. So many nights he'd stayed here after working late, when they could've been together. So many regrets.

Caroline clenched her teeth—there was nothing she could do about the past, whatever mistakes had been made—and squared her shoulders. Miles was relying on her to complete his work.

And plenty of people in the community counted on her help, her leadership, and they'd need that to see them through the difficult times ahead. Starting with the challenges they must be facing at that very moment. No doubt Alvin Fox was stepping into the breach, but while the man might be capable of leading, she felt sure he'd lead them into disaster, given half a chance. For one thing, he didn't know a fraction of what she knew—about the dangers confronting them, that they were sure to face in the future.

Also, she questioned his priorities. She needed to go, leave here and get to wherever citizens would be gathered. So she brushed herself off and stalked out the door into the wider office.

Shaking her head, she remembered what Miles had said before fading away—Verity knew more yet that Caroline would need to know. And the woman was certainly capable of dealing with logistical difficulties. Already a valuable ally, even if Caroline did dislike her, Miss Belue's assistance would be needed even more now.

She had a vague memory of Verity trying to talk to her while she was weeping over Miles, but if that woman had said where she was going or why, Caroline couldn't recall. She had to go back to Miles' office to pick up her purse from the floor where she'd dropped it at some point. Pulling out her pad while leaving again, she saw it still wouldn't connect. The power was back on. So why was the net still down? Verity would know. Likely that's where the woman would be found, dealing with whatever the problem might be.

But Caroline couldn't say *where* that meant she could be found. And clearly couldn't call her to find out. Or anyone else.

Reaching the elevator she paused and wondered whether she should take the stairs instead, and that reminded her of Paul. Macklin had given her a ride here in his cart, but she couldn't remember hearing or seeing him after they'd arrived—where, then, had he gone? And why?

The elevator dinged—she did not recall pushing the button, but she supposed she must have done so —the doors opened and she stepped into the car and shook her head again as they closed. She seemed to be having a difficult time thinking.

Focus, she told herself. She needed to return to the Hall—never should have left, wouldn't have, except she'd been so worried about Miles—which was where everyone would be. Where most of those she needed to talk to would be found, anyway. Certainly that's where Fox would've headed, wherever he'd been when the quake hit. An earthquake. Yes, that was what had happened.

It had killed her husband. And knocked out the power, though that was back on now. With the network down they couldn't communicate, but in spite of all that, she hadn't seen that much actual damage to anything. Or anyone, except for Miles.

She hardly thought it fair a freak accident could take someone so important, so intelligent and alive.

The elevator dinged again and the doors opened. She stepped out into the ground floor lobby, looked around feeling lost for a long moment, then recalled she was headed for the Hall. And she needed to get there fast. Remembering the cart—Paul had driven her here in it, and with power back on it should run alright—she strode to the back exit and out into the night.

The cart was still sitting there near the door but the keys weren't in it. Macklin must've taken those with him. And he must still be inside the building—somewhere, though she didn't know where since he hadn't followed her up to the fifth floor.

She could just walk to the Hall. But that would take a lot longer and leave her less energy when she got there, less able to deal with all she'd have to deal with. And having Paul with her would help.

Heading back into Admin and glancing around the lobby, she tried to imagine where in here Macklin might've gone. Then she realized that while she couldn't call him with her pad, there was a way.

"Paul!" Caroline spun in a circle, calling out his name again and again until she realized he was yelling back at her.

"Are you alright?" The young man, tall with his ebony skin reflecting the bright lights, darted to her side. And from the worried look in his eyes, she had to wonder what she must look like.

She stilled herself and took a deep breath. "No, I'm not. But I have to go on, regardless. And I suppose I'll get better, but right now I need to get to the Hall. We both should go." She grabbed his arm and ushered him toward the back door, not quite sure if she pulled him along or used his arm to steady herself. "Where were you? What were you doing?"

"In the transmission room, working with one of the techs to restore power. We were going over the checklist to make certain there aren't any problems when I heard you hollering."

She nodded. "I'm glad you could help out. But presumably he, or she, doesn't need you anymore."

Paul held the door for her. "No, I'm sure he can handle the rest by himself. And more techs must be on their way." Taking *her* arm he walked her all the way to the cart and settled her in the passenger seat before sliding in behind the wheel.

"Good. Because *I* need you now. To take me to the Hall and help me get things organized. There'll be a lot of work to do." Without the net it would be difficult to assess what needed to be done, prioritize tasks, and assign jobs. But at least with power back on they could make a start. At the Hall.

Many people still thought of the Administration building as the nerve center of the FURC. That had begun to change when the Community Council was expanded, her election as First Councilor had accelerated the shift. Operations were still run from Admin, but the Hall had become the heart of the community.

And there were a lot of important people there, or had been. With power restored some would head home to check on loved ones, but others would head *to* the Hall. Like Alvin Fox. He would definitely get there as quickly as he could. He'd probably already arrived, another reason she needed to get over there as soon as possible.

She started to tell Paul to make the cart go faster, then realized the Hall was already looming up in front of them. The exterior lights blazed, and a few people still stood talking in front of the main doors, but most had likely gone inside. Or left.

Even before Macklin brought the cart to a complete halt, Caroline hopped out and nodded at those milling by the steps. Exchanged greetings, but none of her fellow councilors were there, so she passed by and swiftly took the steps up and strode through the open doors into the lobby.

More people congregated in the main hall—and Alvin was among them. She also spied Tracy Johnson and Jeffrey Minchin. Thankfully all three were separate, talking to different groups of citizens, but then they represented dissimilar constituencies and moved in disparate circles.

Everyone's eyes followed her as she crossed the center of the vast space. Their expressions prodded her to think again about her appearance. Amazingly, she hadn't thought to look in a mirror.

She stopped in the middle of the room and spun around, checking to confirm that Paul had followed her and meeting the gaze of the other three councilors. "I'm calling the council into session. Give me a few minutes to make myself presentable, then we'll meet in the conference room." Her gazed moved to others as she addressed the assembly more generally. "Since the net is down and you can't watch with your pads, I'll come out here and report to everyone once we've finished. It shouldn't take long."

A soft murmuring started up in her wake as she continued toward the back of the hall. She felt Paul stop, letting her go on her own, and she swiftly glided through a door into the back corridor and all the way to her office without encountering anyone else. Thankfully.

Stalking into her small restroom and at last getting a look at herself, Caroline gasped in horror. No wonder people had stared so. Her first inclination was to restore the perfection she assiduously maintained in public. That would take time she couldn't afford to spend, though.

And under the circumstances, she'd do better if they could see she'd been through hell—too bad the net remained down, but with power restored everything in the conference room would be recorded for citizens to watch later at least. Nevertheless, it was necessary to clean herself up a bit. She had said she would, and it wouldn't help if she looked like something the cat dragged in. She would need to radiate authority.

Artfully adjusting her appearance to show them a survivor, somebody who'd been through adversity and overcome it, she turned from the mirror to walk back into the office proper, and her knees wobbled. *Grieve later*, she told herself. For now she'd have to be strong.

Taking a slow, deep breath, she steadied herself and strode out and down the corridor to the conference room. Alvin was already there of course. They all were, and at least he hadn't dared take her place at the head of the table, but he had taken the seat at what would be her right hand. The deputy director usually sat there, but Verity wasn't here—it was too bad Paul hadn't thought to claim it, or moved quick enough.

Still, sitting in his normal place at her left would provide a nice counterbalance to having Fox on her other side. Tracy and Jeffery sat in the next chairs, to stay close she assumed, leaving two empty chairs for the absent Ms. Belue and Dr. Harker at the other end of the table.

Caroline officially opened the meeting and then nodded at Paul. "First, I think we all owe Councilor Macklin here our thanks for helping get power back so soon."

After a general round of thanks, Fox focused his attention on her. "I thought the administration had guaranteed that our power supply wouldn't fail, told us it couldn't."

Clever. With Verity not there, Caroline became the de facto face of the FURC administration, so he was putting her on defense, and she passed the ball to Paul. "Councilor Macklin?"

The student representative nodded, then turned to address Alvin. "The power supply *didn't* fail, but the quake caused faults in the transfer and transmission systems. The repairs were simple and straightforward, but they took a little time since there were only two of us working on it."

He paused, swiveling his head to meet the gazes of the other councilors before continuing. "And now that the system's transmitting electricity again, any receptor nodes damaged in the quake might ignite a fire. The automated suppression systems should put one out if it starts, but a damaged node may mean a building without power."

Tracy started to raise her hand—a bad habit she was trying to strangle—then asked in a tone of confusion, "What exactly does that mean? Will fires be put out or not?"

Fox jumped on that. "You mean there's no way to fight such a fire?"

Thankfully Paul corrected him immediately. "I wouldn't say that. Handheld extinguishers were installed in every building, and the suppression systems can be activated manually. If somebody knows how to."

"But with the network still down, they can't find instructions on their pads, and how many will know what to do on their own?" Alvin's smile was grim.

Caroline jumped in. "Ms. Belue is getting communications restored"—that had to be what she was doing—"and it shouldn't take much longer." Hopefully. "Once our pads can connect, the network will indicate the locations of all system faults."

She looked to Paul, and he nodded in confirmation. "The FURCSnet will inform us what the problems are and where, so we can see they're dealt with immediately."

Caroline smiled her thanks at him, then turned to the others. "Now, while we wait for that, the rest of you can report on the situation here. But first"—she closed her eyes briefly and blew out a big breath—"I have to inform you that Director Miles"—took a moment to 'gather herself' again—"that my husband died from injuries sustained during the quake."

Muted exclamations erupted from every mouth—including Paul's, she should've warned him—and she waved away their condolences. "Ms. Belue, who as his deputy will at least temporarily take his position as director, is already aware of this, but restoring communication has priority. Once she's seen to that, she'll assume her new duties." Presumably. "I thank you for your sympathy and support. And understanding, as I deal with my loss. But it's not only mine, it's everyone's. And the best way to move forward is by taking care of this community."

That should defang Fox, for a while.

Part Three

Delayed Reactions

Chapter 18

False Sense of Security

11:20 p.m. Friday, May 27th
Inside Security Headquarters

BEN POPPED OPEN the microwave to take out the bowl with mostly melted butter and emptied in a pouch of diced power potatoes, sprinkled salt liberally over them and mixed it all up thoroughly with a spoon, then popped the bowl back in the microwave for a quick fry. While nutrition bars were tasty and convenient, real food comforted the stressed soul—especially hot and hearty fare like this—in a way bars never could. He gave thanks again for electricity.

Power had only been back on a couple minutes, and there was work to do, but taking the time to get this quick snack shouldn't do any harm. Susan and Kirkland had left about forty-five minutes ago. Ben had been standing around since, 'holding the fort' as ordered, which had meant standing around and being 'alert' for anyone coming in one of the three unlocked—and, with no power, unlockable—doors into the building. All the lights suddenly flaring back to life had been a huge relief.

And the first thing he'd done was holler at Hope to lock the lobby entrance—knowing both the other doors would lock automatically—so they could relax their vigilance. Chief Nelson still hadn't shown, but he had a key. Anyone else wanting in could knock.

The second thing he'd done was check the net—with his pad as he ran to the break room to melt the butter—and discovered it was still down, despite the power coming back. His primary responsibility was keeping the network secure, but he couldn't do anything about that yet. That left more mundane tasks to take care of.

Ducking down the hall to the lobby, he coughed to get Hope's attention as she stood stretching near the duty desk. "With the lights on, we should check to see if the building sustained any damage." By the dim red glow they hadn't been able to see clearly to assess things properly, and he knew that was something they should do now. "You take this floor, and I'll inspect upstairs."

She stared meaningfully at the spoon in his hand, just as the microwave dinged in the distance.

Ben gave her a sheepish grin. "I can eat while I look, can't I?" He started back for the break room—the intoxicating aroma had already wafted this far—and spoke over his shoulder. "Just make sure to log what you find on your pad." The net might be down at the moment, but as soon as it was back up, those reports would be accessible, and someone else could decide what needed to be fixed and when. And presumably *by* somebody else.

She called out after him. "I think I smell something burning."

But when he reached the microwave, he popped it open to find his potatoes fried to perfection. If an acrid tang of smoldering metal still lingered faintly, the microwave itself was responsible for that.

Taking the hot bowl in one hand, he walked out shoveling home fries into his mouth with his spoon in the other hand. Down the hall, then up the stairs, he chewed carefully as he examined the walls, looking for cracks, he supposed, or any kind of damage. Anything visible to the naked eye.

He saw a piece of plaster lying shattered on the carpet, then glanced up to see it had fallen from the ceiling. But that was little enough destruction, considering what that quake had felt like.

Shaking his head as he reached the second floor and found nothing out of place there in the corridor, he went first into the Resource Room and examined his workstation. It still wouldn't connect to the net, of course. The second the system came back online, his pad would alert him to the fact—he'd programed it to do that. But otherwise everything seemed to be operating alright.

He wondered what was actually wrong with the network. The servers would have rebooted by now. If they could. Perhaps the quake had broken something in the communications relay or damaged part of the wider array. Unfortunately, he could not find out without going over to the Admin building. Onto the roof. He doubted he'd want to even if he could. And he had his orders.

Behind the aroma of home fries he thought he could still detect a whiff of scorched metal. Leaning toward the equipment and sniffing, he knew it came from somewhere else, but glancing around the room revealed nothing else that might account for it. So that smell had to be merely an olfactory memory. Or his imagination.

He shoveled in the last of the potatoes, then set the bowl and spoon on the table and walked out. In the hall he faced the door to the Chief's private area with embarrassment and almost choked on the last bite of home fries. The boss didn't live in his rooms up here anymore, but still...

Ben had to be thorough, and better him looking around in there than Hope. Swallowing that last of his hasty meal, he opened the door just as the lights went out again. He bit back a rare swear word. Life had just returned to normal—mostly—and he didn't want to go back to being without electricity. And he didn't like being alone in the dark.

The dim red glow of the emergency lights gradually came up, but they really didn't help much. He heard Hope yelling something downstairs, couldn't make out the words, but could guess pretty well she was as upset as him about the new blackout. Whatever was going on with the power, there wasn't anything either of them could do about it. They'd have to go back to standing around, or sitting, and 'holding the fort' while waiting for Chief Nelson to arrive or the power to come back on, again.

Whichever came first. Ben started for the stairs but stopped as the burning smell returned, stronger than ever. And then it hit him.

There must've been damage, to the node which received electricity wirelessly, or to the regular insulated copper wires that conducted it throughout the building. And when the power had returned, it had started a fire somewhere. Which must have caused the circuit breaker to cut off the electricity. Was the node still receiving power? That would feed the fire and mean disaster. Had the sensors detected a fire? The alert would've needed the net working to sound on their pads, and that was down.

Had the automatic suppression system activated? The growing stench of smoke said he had to assume it hadn't, but he felt paralyzed, couldn't think what he needed to do.

Then a dark shape barreled at him from the top of the stairs. Knocked him to the ground as it went into the Resource Room. Only, it had been a person rather than an 'it'. Not Hope, but somebody larger, and Ben hoped that whoever it was they were racing to fight the fire. He himself felt quite useless.

Nevertheless. Picking himself up off the carpet and brushing himself off, he walked in to offer what help he could. And was shoved to the ground again as the person ran back out. This time, though, he'd gotten a good look at the shadowed face and knew—it had been Brandon Radley. Just the same as every other non-supervisory officer, Ben had to work routine shifts at the detention center. And was familiar with the faces of their most infamous prisoners.

This time he shouted a strong curse, so unusual for him he knew it would have shocked anyone who heard. Maybe Hope had—if she was alive to hear—except he could guess now what she'd been screaming about a minute ago. Scrambling to his feet, Ben raced back out and down the stairs, almost tripping as he went. Heard one of the doors banging shut as he reached the first floor. And hoped it was the exit being slammed.

The side door, he thought, but it was weird how sound traveled sometimes, so he couldn't be certain—and he wouldn't go chasing after the man, even if he were sure. Instead, he ran toward the lobby and collided with Hope heading his way.

Short but somewhat chubby, she had a good ten pounds on him and almost bowled Ben over, but he held on to her and stayed upright. This time. "You alright?" He looked her over and she seemed okay.

"I asked who he was, tried to stop him when he just pushed past, but he threw me to the ground."

Ben sighed. "But you're alright now?"

Nodding, she stepped back, then looked him in the eye. "But what should we do? I mean—"

He never found out what she meant, because he suddenly remembered the fire and cut her off. "The building's on fire. Grab that extinguisher under the duty desk, then look around for flames down here. I can get the one from the break room and head back upstairs." Where the fire actually seemed to be, but he didn't want Hope dealing with any smoke.

Awareness had dawned on her face as he spoke—even if she didn't know why a fire had started, she knew one had, and she'd already turned and strode back into the lobby before he finished. As he headed to the break room, he thought furiously. The fire suppression system could be activated manually. If he could remember how.

And the power node for headquarters was up in the ceiling somewhere. That explained why the fire had apparently begun upstairs, but he'd have a hard time using an extinguisher to fight flames up in the rafters. Regardless, he took the one from the break room and climbed back to the second floor. As fast as his weary feet could carry him.

Reaching the landing, he pulled the collar of his shirt over his mouth to keep out most of the smoke, which he could see now, even in the dim red illumination. He plunged into the Resource Room, but he didn't find any flames, though the haze was making it more difficult to see as well as to breathe.

Then his gaze fell on the metal panel set high on the back wall and remembered. He darted over to it and yanked it open, burning his fingers as he did, to find what he was hoping for. And neatly labeled.

Flipping the switch that started the suppression system, he heard the hiss of foam pouring out. And gave a sigh of relief as he sank to the floor.

At least he'd managed that much. And Brandon hadn't got his hands on what he'd been looking for. Ben glanced over at the huge safe that was their armory, that *didn't* automatically unlock when power failed. But he'd let a dangerous fugitive escape. He had failed.

11:20 p.m. Friday, May 27th
Inside the Detention Center

MICHELLE MORI SIGHED and turned to gesture at Greg Belaford, and the junior officer opened the door to the men's ward and held it open for her. As soon as the lights had come back on, she'd taken a medical kit and headed in here to examine the inmates Sara King had incapacitated. The three male prisoners first, then she'd planned to go over to the women's ward and see Marigold, since she had only been able to give any of them a cursory examination by the dim glow of the emergency lights. Even with a little light from her pad helping.

But that had been enough to show her that former officer King had 'done a number' on all four, so Michelle wanted another, better look at them.

The power had just gone out again though, only a couple minutes or so after it had returned. Denying her the opportunity. This hazy red illumination made re-examining the injured prisoners pointless. And she felt uneasy about remaining on the ward in the dark, with most cell doors once again unlocked.

The three hard cases were no threat—aside from barely being able to move, their cells had been padlocked shut. And the others had behaved fairly well after the earlier commotion, obediently returning to their cells and settling down for the night. But with only Greg Belaford there, she felt unsafe.

She sighed again, this time with relief, when the door closed off the ward behind them. Even though it wouldn't lock, so that feeling of reprieve was irrational. "Perhaps we should barricade the doors, the ones to the wards."

Her partner merely shrugged. "Just the ones in back or the doors leading to the lobby as well? And with what? We'd be hard-pressed to find enough to block the doors that let back to the staff section. At least they'll think twice before trying to escape after what Sara did."

Shaking her head, Michelle rued having such an inexperienced officer as her only backup. Resented having to work the occasional shift at the detention center, come to that. With the resumption of FedU classes close to three years ago, she had been able to complete her criminalistics classes as well as all her pre-med coursework. She was now a fully qualified forensic technician and was due to soon start training to become a doctor. Granted there wasn't much call for a criminalist here, babysitting this bunch of delinquents was surely a waste of her time.

David Belue was right—most infractions people were detained for didn't warrant incarceration, and those individuals need not be held while waiting for adjudication, could face other punishments besides being shut up in here for however many weeks. But the worst offenders should be expelled. No one who would attack anyone unprovoked, who would attack a security officer, was ever going to be a citizen who contributed to the community. They would have to be held in custody until that determination could be made, but the three small cells at Security HQ were sufficient for that. Or should be. Then there would be no need for any officers to work these shifts.

Michelle suspected Paul Macklin thought so too—he'd never said anything outright, but some of the questions he'd asked...

Perhaps they could get him to press the issue in a council session. She was considering what would be the best approach for her and David to take with Paul when her partner pushed the break room door open and waved her in ahead of him. She started to step inside and stopped, staring into an inferno.

At least, she saw hazy smoke hanging in the red glow of the emergency lights and drifting out of the open doorway. And flames licking their way up the back wall.

Coughing, Greg dashed into the room and took a handheld extinguisher from where it was clipped on the side of a cupboard. Then—holding an arm over his face—he started spraying foam on the fire. And his muffled voice called back at her. "You'll have to evacuate the prisoners." Again.

Although they'd spent over half an hour getting the detainees back into the building, into their cells and settled down—and despite her being the senior officer here—she nodded. "I'll get them moving. As soon as you're done here though, come through and give me a hand." Hopefully Greg Belaford would be able to contain the flames, but once he'd done what he could—successful or not—he would have to help. They couldn't take chances with the inmates' lives.

Better if they escaped than get trapped inside a burning building. Even those four hard cases—they didn't deserve to die, much less suffer such a horrible death—though the thought of them, loose in the compound, terrorizing people trying to deal with an already awful situation, was also abhorrent. How to deal with them was a difficult question.

The others, the ones not padlocked in their own cells, could be reasoned with. Offer them a choice—the carrot or the stick.

Entering the women's ward first, she called out to the eight inmates sitting or standing in their cells as they murmured to each other, no doubt wondering what was going on. "We're evacuating you from the building again." There were eight prisoners left—not counting Marigold—and she considered their various personalities. "I'm dividing you into groups of four." She separated them into two different sets as they exited their cells, in a way she at least hoped would minimize the risk of confrontation. Or collusion.

"You will each be held responsible for how every member of your group behaves. Follow orders, stay in the Yard unless instructed otherwise, and refrain from attacking anyone—and I'll see you're rewarded for it. But if one of you causes trouble, the others in the group will receive the same punishment." Their sullen looks showed they understood. "Now, march out through the lobby in an orderly fashion."

The eight women obeyed swiftly enough, if a bit grudgingly, and as soon as she saw they weren't going to argue about it, Michelle turned and grimaced at Marigold still lying on her cot in a padlocked cell. "I'll come back for you in a few minutes."

As she walked out and headed over to the men's ward, she hoped they would be similarly compliant. With three in bad shape and two having already escaped, that left nine male prisoners she could divide into three groups of three and give the same orders to. And offer the same terms.

She also wondered how best to deal with the inmates in those padlocked cells. They weren't in any shape to cause much trouble, but she'd still want to zip-tie them again before dragging them out. She'd need Greg Belaford's help with that for sure.

Walking back onto the men's ward, she saw the detainees had remained in their cells. And the nine she wanted were all awake and sitting on their cots, talking to each other in low voices. Their conversation cut off as they noticed her entrance. As soon as she got them organized and on their way out of this building, she'd go back and see how Greg was faring in his battle with the fire.

Chapter 19

Racing on Ahead

11:30 p.m. Friday, May 27th
Northeast section of the buffer zone

KAT RAN ACROSS the uneven grass, making up for the slower pace she'd been forced to take before the lights suddenly banished the night. A couple of spotlights mounted behind and above the perimeter wall had been dark—they must've been damaged by the seismic wave and blown when the power returned—but most shone like little suns out over the buffer zone and past the slanting security fence, pushing a fair distance into the black wilderness beyond. That should do something to keep the predators away.

Still being unable to connect to the net—unable to communicate with anyone while she was alone in the buffer zone—frustrated her, and made her want to run faster. But the broken ground kept her from going as fast as she could, even with the light.

At least the motion detectors she knew she was setting off wouldn't be driving people crazy sending out alerts while the net was down. And not needing to avoid those meant moving more quickly. As long as she didn't encounter any further obstacles.

As far as wild animals went, a lone panther had been tentatively trying to find a way over one bowed section of fence—inexplicably leaning inward there, and she'd had to bend down to avoid the razor wire hanging in the air—but she'd scared that big cat off. By making a lot of noise, not her usual style.

Now the way was mostly clear as well as bright, and she'd covered a good bit of ground over the last quarter hour or so. And she sensed somebody running toward her long before she could hear the person breathing hard from exertion, much less sneakers brushing through blades of grass.

Then Patience came careening around the curve up ahead. Kat had already slowed down, not knowing what was headed her way, but the other girl had failed to notice her until she was getting close, then skidded to a halt a few feet from where Kat stopped to wait.

"What are you doing here on your own?" If Patience had been patrolling with a partner, had that other guard been injured? Was the girl running toward the back gate for help? She was too new to be prepared to handle a crisis like this, even if she was Ken's daughter. "What's wrong?"

Patience shook her head and took a deep breath before answering. "The two patrolling this section—I was on the front gate and got selected to be sent—they're alright, just slow. As soon as I'd given them the message, I ran on ahead. They'll be here before too long."

"What message?" Kat bit back a harsh word for the girl who was, after all, still learning. "From Sgt. MacTierney?" Tim was supervising the guards this shift, and he'd probably been at the gate.

"Yeah, he sent me along this stretch while going up the western half of the buffer zone himself. But I should be asking you what *you're* doing here. After all, it's your anniversary, isn't it? And here you are, on your own, when you should be snuggled up with that handsome hubby of yours in one of dad's luxury suites."

Kat gritted her teeth. Did the girl actually think she'd stay huddled away when the FURC was facing a disaster like this. "The message? What was so urgent the sergeant sent you, a raw recruit, racing—on your own, all alone—up the buffer zone in the midst of a crisis like this?"

Patience grinned. "Well, he knows I'm fast and wanted to get the guards at the back gate some help as soon as possible. So he told me to catch up to the patrol and tell them to get a move on, hurry up and reinforce Grace and Wagner, and once I had I raced on ahead of them. In the spirit of the message, even if it wasn't in the letter of my orders." Her grin grew wider. "I'm not in trouble, am I?"

Of course, wanting to help whoever had wound up at the back gate when the quake had hit was the reason Kat had headed there herself. She shouldn't be surprised Tim had thought of the need too, especially since he'd have known Grace would be one of them. "No, you're not in trouble." Though Kat had an issue with the girl's intrusive interest in her personal life, that wasn't an 'official' problem. "But I'm afraid the guard hut collapsed and killed Wagner. I left Grace at the back gate on her own."

She shouldn't have, but she was still sometimes a bit hasty. Not as bad as Patience, this inappropriately named young woman. Surely she'd never been so rash. "If the regular patrol is alright and on their way, I should start back now. And be quick."

The youngest Cameron daughter started to nod before she finished speaking and darted past on the word 'quick'. Wanted to reach her eldest sister fast, apparently.

Kat turned and ran after her. And Patience hollered back over her shoulder. "Oh, and father broke his leg. He's well enough otherwise, I hear, but like a bear with a sore tooth I imagine. And he put Carruthers in charge at headquarters. Sgt. MacTierney is officially in command at the front gate, but he left Lacey supervising things there."

Because he wanted to go to Grace himself. Kat could understand that, but she'd have to have a talk with Tim about putting personal concerns ahead of duty. She'd have to pray for Ken. And then as soon as there were enough guards to secure the back gate, she needed to get to headquarters.

11:35 p.m. Friday, May 27th
Northwest section of the buffer zone

TIM PUSHED HARDER now that the lights on the wall helped him see the ground beneath his feet better. He'd hated leaving Hodges behind, but with that sprained ankle it would have slowed him down too much. And with Alvarez to watch Hodge's back and help the man hobble his way to the front gate—hopefully without too much trouble—the debilitated guard should get medical attention soon enough.

Tim would've like to bring them both along with him to the north gate. Grace might need more help than what MacTierney alone could provide after all. But more important was reaching her fast and finding out she was alive and well. Of course she had to be, but he needed to see it to fully believe it.

Knowing she could take care of herself, far better than he could himself, didn't stop him worrying about her. She wasn't immortal, none of them were immune to immolation. Or being crushed by a falling wall. Or—

He stumbled, somehow kept from falling again, and ran on. Forced himself to stop imagining every dire fate that might have befallen her—there was no way he could change what might have happened already, and it didn't help him reach her any faster. A sprained ankle was the last thing he needed.

Instead he wondered whether she worried over what might've happened to him. It wouldn't be like her to be concerned. About anything really, and he wished he could be more like that, even as he hoped she was at least a little worried about him.

Shaking his head, he tried to focus on the earth beneath his feet and pay attention to the path ahead of him as he lengthened his stride. And gave thanks again for the light. It not only helped him, it should help her and Wagner as well, whatever trouble they might be facing at the back gate. If only the net had come back online at the same time.

He'd checked right away, of course, in the hope of calling Grace and finding out she was alright that much sooner. Had thought about sending a text regardless, to tell her he was on his way—it would get sent automatically the second a connection could be made—but he didn't want to stop and type it out. It wouldn't help him anyway, and he doubted it would help her either. Might distract her, even.

Come to think of it, calling her might not be the brightest idea, not knowing what she might be dealing with at any given moment. All the more reason to run.

Any thought of noting damage to the fence and the wall had long gone out the window, but it could wait. Would have to wait. But since the lights were on, the cameras mounted along the wall ought to be working too, and once the net was up, people could pan those around to assess the damage to the fence. And as far as he'd seen, the wall only had cracks.

Just after he had that thought, the curving view ahead of him revealed a gap at the top, where some bricks had broken off and crumbled to the ground—not enough to constitute a major breach, but something that would have to be repaired right away.

And a little beyond that section of the wall, Tim saw the gate in the security fence. Though it leaned almost to the ground, the sight made his heart leap, because it meant he'd almost reached Grace. Razor wire hung suspended a few feet above the grass and a few away from the wall. It compelled him to slow down so he could safely squeeze through. *Soon.*

He called out as he came, with the loudest voice he could manage under the circumstances. "Grace! Wagner!" That last because he didn't want to sound unprofessional, even though he couldn't care less if that lazy guard was alright. If that man had let anything happen to Grace while working with her, Tim would do something drastic. Didn't know what, but hopefully it wouldn't be necessary. "Grace!"

Then he saw the wrought-iron gate, and Grace's head poking out and staring back at him. "Be quiet, you fool." She was yelling herself, but Tim couldn't complain—not now. Not ever, actually, which was a good reason he shouldn't even nominally be her supervisor, but that was also a problem for tomorrow. Or the day after.

Since she was clearly okay, he took his time the rest of the way. And the space between the wall and the razor wire suddenly seemed much wider. However, when he actually reached the gate, he found it frozen partway open with only a narrow gap he had to squeeze through.

He had to pass his handgun and rifle through to Grace, then suck in his stomach and scrape between the concrete pillar and the wrought-iron bar, which didn't do much for the state of his uniform. Though it had already looked the worse for wear. No doubt he looked pretty rough himself, and Grace was patting him down like she was looking for holes.

Maybe she *had* been worried. "So where's Wagner?" He asked as she gave him a second examination.

"Dead. The guard hut collapsed on him."

Tim took her by the shoulders and just stopped himself from shaking her. "That could just as easily have been you."

Grace gave him a flat stare. "But it wasn't."

"And he left you on your own here."

She shook her head. "It's been quiet ever since. And Lt. Miles showed up a while back, then took off down the east side of the buffer zone."

Tim nodded. "To check on the guards who'd be headed here, I suppose." And leaving Grace on her own again, even though there were always supposed to be two guards posted here. But policy apparently didn't apply to the lieutenant. "She'll run into your sister Patience, I expect." That reminded him what he had to tell her. "And your father somehow broke his leg in the quake." The chief had not volunteered any details of how that had happened, and Cameron wasn't a man you questioned. "Don't know how bad it is, but bad enough to put him out of action."

Before she could respond to that—assuming she would have—Lt. Miles and Patience came racing up to the gate on the buffer zone side. Grace's younger sister slid through the gap with ease, but at least the lieutenant had to remove her shoulder holster, then wiggle her way between. For some reason Grace hit him on the arm.

Lt. Miles grimaced at him. “You shouldn’t have come yourself, but I guess I’m glad you’re here. After the slow pokes following us get here, you’ll have four guards to defend this gate. And I can leave you in charge and head to HQ.”

“Yes, Lieutenant.” She’d already turned away to have a quiet word with Grace, and all he could think about was the awkwardness. And how the time had come to talk to Chief Cameron about the man’s eldest daughter. A conversation he’d been dreading.

Chapter 20

In the Nick of Time

11:35 p.m. Friday, May 27th
Approaching the Detention Center

OFFICER COURDRAY PUSHED the captured fugitive ahead of her down the walkway, fighting an increasing sense of frustration. With his hands tied behind him, Hennessey couldn't walk fast, not safely anyway. But the sullen delinquent had made the going slower than it had to be, dragging his feet and making her prod him to take each step. Stumbling, now and then, so she had to pull him back before he fell.

Urging him on again, Lisa was grateful she had gone beyond the more populated areas, where people had been wandering about, complaining to each other. And giving her strange looks.

As soon as power had been restored, to provide plenty of light outside to see by, she had decided to return the escaped prisoner to the detention center. That's where he belonged, not tied to the railing beside the steps to the Roses' front door. And she had nothing better to do.

The houses in their middle-class neighborhood hadn't sustained any substantial damage. Her little Joey—the excitement of all the shaking long past as well as his usual bedtime—had zonked out and been carried to one of the Roses' guest bedrooms. There wouldn't have been much point to her carrying him home to put in his own bed, not after Mrs. Rose had volunteered to take care of him. And not much use Lisa going home alone.

So she had begun this long slog across the compound, pushing and pulling and dragging this stubborn, uncooperative prisoner the entire way. Since she couldn't call it in and have officers who *were* on duty come and take him back in a cart. Neither had she had the luck to run into any of them. But finally she'd come within sight of her goal, spotting the security fence around the detention center up ahead.

As they got closer, she could see several prisoners milling about in the Yard between the fence and the front of the building, but even squinting did not reveal either of the officers who should be watching them.

No surprise they'd evacuated the inmates. They must be worried about the integrity of the structure. And then, with power out the cell doors would have unlocked—all the doors, in fact—and there wouldn't be much point to keeping them inside. And the two on duty here would have their hands full.

Having been off duty herself, Lisa was having a hard time recalling just who those two would be, but the bigger question was—where were they? More to the point, why hadn't they returned the detainees to their cells? Power had come back more than twenty minutes ago.

Unfortunately, the closer he got to the gate, the more Hennessey resisted moving forward. Lisa had to get a bit rough with him.

Fortunately, she had taken her security key with her—she made sure to always have it on her, a habit which now turned out to be useful—so even though the net was still down she was able to use her pad to unlock the gate in the fence.

Even better, those prisoners closest to the fence moved away as they saw her unlock the gate. She'd been worried they might try to rush her in the hope of escaping, and she wasn't armed—always carrying her gun would've been a good habit to keep up. But as peaceful as this place had grown in the past three years, somehow she'd gotten out of it. At least when she was off duty.

Tonight had been a timely reminder that a cop, of any kind, was always on duty. And if wearing her gun upset some of the other mothers, so be it.

Shoving Jake through the open gate, she looked at the several small groups of prisoners and counted only seventeen detainees, when there ought to have been twenty-three, after accounting for the one she was bringing back. The missing six had presumably escaped as he had. The remaining inmates stood in two groups of four women and three groups of three men, each cluster keeping far apart from the others —and there had to be a reason for that. But she was just glad they kept their distance from her while she relocked the gate.

Hennessey sank to his knees, and she looked at the closest knot of women. “Where are Officers Mori and Belaford?” As she needed to ask she'd remembered it was Michelle and Greg who'd been assigned this shift at the detention center.

The one with the thick braid—Becky—answered quickly. “Inside. Fighting the fire. And they'd better be trying to get the others out.”

At the word ‘fire’, Lisa had headed for the lobby at a run and just managed to hear that last, and had to wonder why they hadn't evacuated everybody together. Then she was through the doors.

Power was out inside, only that dim emergency lighting to see anything by, but despite the red glow to confuse things, there clearly wasn't any fire here. Or any people.

Continuing through the intake room for female detainees and onto the women's ward, she discovered Michelle dragging a zip-tied prisoner along on one of the thin mattresses. Marigold, who'd apparently caused trouble and had to be subdued—rather thoroughly by the look of her. "Let me help you."

Michelle glanced over her shoulder as she heard her voice, as Lisa moved forward to take one corner of the bed. "No, I've got this, but there are more injured inmates on the men's ward. And Greg is back in the break room trying to contain a fire." And the slightly built woman continued tugging her burden down the hall in the direction of the lobby.

Lisa ran around her. "Got it." Sprinted toward the far door, found the corridor beyond empty, then raced to the break room to see Greg waving a handheld extinguisher at the back wall, which was nearly half covered with flames. But only pathetic puffs of foam spat from the nozzle.

He tossed the empty canister to the ground and swore, then turned and noticed her presence behind him. "That was the last. They're all used up now. I slowed the spread, but there's nothing more anyone can do. Except help Michelle get the others out."

Nodding, Lisa looked around. "You already activated the suppression system and it didn't work?"

Seeing his jaw drop in shock, she darted across into the kitchen and scanned the wall for the circuit breaker panel. Behind her she heard him shouting, "But, the power..."

"It can be activated manually, even if the power is out." Finding the shallow metal cabinet and pulling it open, she flipped the switch. She heard foam hissing in the walls, saw it start spraying from overhead nozzles, and sighed with relief. "But we'll still need to get everyone out. Help me with those male prisoners."

The thought of more work when she'd had such a long, difficult day—and evening—and was actually off duty, that didn't improve her mood, nor the fact that Greg hadn't known to activate the suppression system. Or that it could be done manually. Though she had eventually found her kid, and that gave her great relief, she could really use a break. But clearly she wasn't going to get one anytime soon.

Four injured inmates and the fugitive she'd just returned meant there were two prisoners still unaccounted for, and no way to warn anybody while the net remained down. And no doubt there were more problems yet she wasn't aware of, plenty of trouble, just waiting around the next corner. But that was a cop's life.

11:35 p.m. Friday, May 27th
In the middle of the Green

SUSAN LISTENED WITH amusement as Salazar tried to defend his decision to Kirkland. "There may be a need for him at the clinic or not, we don't know, but—"

The Deputy Chief of Internal Security cut off an excuse they'd already heard with a snort. "Yes, lots of people here needing first aid, from the quake and some scuffles that came after. Because you couldn't keep this lot in line." He held up a hand to stop any interruption. "I know, there was only you and Gabe to maintain order, and power out and all..."

Even walking, she and Kirkland had reached the northwest 'corner' of the Green shortly before lights had sprung to life all around, revealing a hundred or more citizens milling about on the grass. As well as Salazar and Gabe in the distance confronting a very angry man who turned out to be a surgeon they had drafted into tending to the injured, who was objecting to being kept there against his will when he was urgently needed at the clinic. Or so he claimed.

With the net down, no one could know for sure what the situation was anywhere else, or who might be needed where. But as soon as they'd reached the scene and heard his complaint, Kirkland had taken the surgeon's side. "Seems to me you and Gabe can give first aid to anyone who needs it, since you have the necessary training."

The Deputy Chief had then turned to the doctor with a fixed look. "And I know you won't mind asking your wife"—who was a nurse—"to stay and continue lending a hand."

The surgeon had swallowed the objection forming on his lips and grudgingly nodded. "Of course." He must've seen the wisdom of taking the win while he could. "As long as she's needed here. But they'll want her help at the clinic after that."

"Sure. It probably won't be long before she follows you there, and I'll make sure she gets an escort to see she arrives safely."

Kirkland now stared at Salazar. "It'll be safer if people stay here until we have a better idea of what exactly's going on. But with the power back on, any who want to leave, maybe check on their loved ones —we should let them go. With a warning to be careful of course." There likely wouldn't be many left to manage once they'd been told that.

The shift supervisor nodded in acquiescence. "I will see that message is spread. And now that power is back and our cart will run again, perhaps once things are settled here Gabe and I should go back on patrol. Find anyone else who needs our help. With your permission, sir."

But Kirkland shook his head. "You're giving the cart to Susan, so she can run the doctor here over to the medical center lickety-split." He turned to her. "Get him there as swiftly as you safely can."

He gestured at Salazar to hand the keys over to her, and she quickly grabbed the surgeon by the arm and led him off toward the cart. And as they strode across the grass, she heard her boss continue. "Now you've got me to help you organize things here, and as soon as I think we've got it all under control, you can walk Mrs. Laurie here over to the clinic and collect your cart and go back on patrol."

Susan imagined Salazar fuming. And biting his tongue, since he had little choice in what to do with the Deputy Chief right there giving orders. But she needed to concentrate on her own task. Despite the lights blazing everywhere, there were still shadows, and the ground broken enough to trip the unwary—she had to keep the doctor from harm as well as herself, so she needed to focus. She could chuckle over Salazar getting set down later, at her leisure. With a glass of wine.

Once she'd settled the surgeon in the passenger seat of the car and slipped behind the wheel, Susan gave him a warm smile—he was handsome even if a married man—then started cautiously driving along the walkway. Now it was cracks in the cement she'd have to watch for, but she got up a good speed.

Once she reached the circular pavement circling the Green, she turned onto the path that weaved its way around the east side of Admin. And laughed to herself. Her day off and having to work all evening. But needed for nothing except escorting various VIP citizens around the compound.

Not that she was complaining. But it wasn't far to the medical center, especially at this speed, and if she was supposed to leave the cart at the clinic to be picked up by Gabe and Salazar later, then what was she meant to do after she dropped off the doctor?

Maybe by then the net would be back up. Then Chief Nelson would be giving the orders, supposing he was alive and able. But nothing she'd seen so far suggested there'd been any fatalities or even serious injuries.

And if communications had *not* been restored—well then, she'd just have to take a look around and see for herself. Surely somebody somewhere would need help.

Chapter 21

Alive, Awake, Alert

11:40 p.m. Friday, May 27th
First floor of the FURC Medical Center

DAVID SAT PRAYING in the waiting room outside the surgical suite, where Amita had left him an awful long time ago, sitting on one of the hard plastic seats he found just as uncomfortable as it looked to be. Although the circumstances would have kept him from relaxing regardless.

Ken's blood pressure had been dropping too far and too fast—even with the fluids they'd been giving him—to wait for one of the surgeons to show up. So Amita had told him she had no choice but to take on the job herself.

She'd seemed reluctant but also confident. And David kept reminding himself how smart and capable she was. And if she'd been rusty, she had gotten plenty of practice already this evening—though that thought brought to mind how tired she'd looked.

The swush of the doors to the operating theater opening prompted him to raise his head in hope. A far more exhausted Amita came out and gave him a weak smile. "He'll live. He lost a lot of blood, but I was able to repair all the damaged vessels in his injured leg. We're giving him plasma to replace what he lost, and the man's got the constitution of an ox. That's the good news."

David braced himself. "That sounds like there's some bad news too." But Ken was going to live.

She nodded wearily and plopped down hard on the seat beside him. "He suffered a compound fracture to his femur, which is bad enough. But he also smashed up his knee something terrible—you don't want the technical terms, I know. It's beyond me to repair him. Even with the work of a talented orthopedic surgeon—which we happen to have, if he ever gets here—Chief Cameron probably won't be able to walk right the rest of his life. I'm just hopeful—"

"Sounds like I'm just in time." A tall, handsome fellow in an expensive suit strode in with one of the sisters and Susan Wellman close on his heels. "He's still on the operating table?"

"Yes. And I'm glad to see you, Dr. Laurie. Your patient has—"

The man cut her off with a wave of his hand as he walked past her toward the wide swinging doors. "I got the gist, but I like to see for myself. Doctor. I had better scrub up now and get in there. The sooner I start the better the results." And then he'd gone through, with the nurse following right behind.

Amita shrugged and smiled. "He's the best, really. Chief Cameron couldn't be in better hands."

Susan shook her head. "That man is arrogance on steroids, but if he's even half as good as he thinks he is..." She shrugged. "I'm just glad to have delivered him, to be done with the—" Whatever she was going to call him, she stopped herself.

David sighed with relief. His friend would live, and they'd fix him up the best they could. And with the changes caused by the Lift Virus still unfolding, even the experts no longer tried to say what was and wasn't possible. So he bet Ken would not only walk again, but be more active than ever.

He felt Susan slap his arm. "Don't just sit there and mope, man. Best thing to do is keep busy. And I'm sure there's plenty we could be doing out there." She pulled him out of the chair and began dragging him away. "I don't suppose you've got a cart?"

Nodding, he considered his priorities. "I need a cup of coffee." Thank God the power was back on.

Chapter 21

11:45 p.m. Friday, May 27th
The rooftop of the Administration Building

VERITY STARED INTO a vast blackness dotted with pinpricks of light, felt as if she were floating in space. Until she felt the cold concrete pressing into her shoulder blades. Realized she was lying on that hard, damp surface and remembered where she had been before blacking out. What she'd been doing as well.

A soft glow surrounded the edges of her peripheral vision, lightening the dark of the night, and she suddenly understood that the power had returned—must've come back on while she was touching those parallel switches. She'd electrocuted herself.

With a sigh she struggled to sit up, heart racing—she would have to get them to check her out at the clinic, but later—and looked around her. Found she was alone on the roof and in relative dark. Reached for her pad to turn on the lights up here before realizing she couldn't. Not until she finished fixing that communications relay.

But first things first. She felt around until she'd found where her pad had fallen, thumbed it back on and sighed again to find it still worked. With power transmitting now, she didn't have to worry anymore about the battery running down either.

Getting her feet under her, she finally managed to stand and stagger over to where the communications relay box still sat gaping open. Shining a light from her pad into the cavity, she confirmed that the next to last circuit board had been correctly fitted in its slot—that was the one she'd just finished inspecting, had been snapping back in when...

That was where her memory ended, but at least she'd got that last board back in properly as she was losing consciousness. And hadn't done any damage as far as she could see. One more circuit board still lay askew—that would have to be carefully checked, and repaired if necessary, before being replaced.

Before starting that examination, though, Verity wanted to see about the servers. Walking over to the panel and pulling it down, she saw the diagnostic routine had completed with no errors discovered and the system had automatically rebooted as soon as main power had been restored. A notice had appeared on the screen informing her—and a flashing light off to one side indicated the very same thing—that the communications relay was offline, preventing the program from establishing network connections. Which she already knew.

She put those servers back to sleep so they'd be ready to reboot again, then began the laborious and tedious routine of shutting down the array. Once it was powered down she'd be able to go back to work on the relay without the risk of giving herself another shock. If she'd done this to begin with, she would have saved some time as well as avoided an electrocution. But she'd thought she had enough time. No use regretting a decision, though, that she could not take back.

Even time travel didn't afford a person that opportunity. Or so she'd been told.

Well, she thought, as she concentrated on what she was doing, if that last circuit board that needed checking was undamaged—and the others had been fine, so it probably would be too—it should not take too long to get the network back up. If she focused, stopped letting her mind wander from her work.

11:50 p.m. Friday, May 27th
The Community Council Conference Room

CAROLINE CUT OFF discussion of how to handle any fires that broke out, once they learned about them. "I think we've gone over everything we know about the situation"—which was little enough—"and what steps we can take until the net is back up." To death, it seemed, though they had only been talking ten or fifteen minutes. More than enough. "I move we adjourn so I can update the people waiting in the main hall." She'd promised them that and couldn't afford to delay addressing them any longer.

Paul immediately seconded the motion, and she was grateful for his unhesitating support, gave him a warm smile before nodding to the others and rising from her chair. She stretched to work out the kinks that had formed in the short time she'd been sitting there, then passed behind Paul and Tracy. Through the door and down the hall. To the door at the back of the hall, where she paused and prepared to show them the widow who'd submerged grief so she could do what needed to be done. Then walked in.

The crowd had grown in size in the fifteen minutes or so since she'd left them. Climbing the steps onto the speaking platform, she scanned their faces and realized several people had left—to be replaced by others, by more for sure, but those missing individuals must have headed home. To check on loved ones, belongings, or just to see if they still had a bed to sleep in.

The new faces would be those who'd left behind circumstances that must've been alright, been close enough to reach the Hall in such a short time. Who had taken advantage of the lights on throughout the compound to make their way here in hopes of finding out what they couldn't with their pads—what in the world was going on. And she had precious little to tell them.

"First, I know we're all rattled. No one expected that quake or power going out—we thought we were safe from those things at least. Thankfully the power and lights are back on, so we can see what we are doing, but with the net still down it's difficult to assess the extent of the damage we've suffered."

Citizens shuffled their feet, with a few murmuring softly to someone standing next to them, but no one interrupted. "Though I do have some information for you. First, I hate to tell you, Director Jonathan Miles died this evening from injuries sustained in the quake. My husband was a visionary. And the dream he realized through the creation of the FURC is why we've enjoyed relative peace and prosperity." She wiped a tear from the corner of her eye. "As the world around us has rapidly fallen apart. So please take a moment with me to silently give thanks. And remember a great man who worked hard for us all." Even if most hadn't appreciated it at the time.

Turning her head to gaze across the crowd, trying to meet every eye, Caroline continued. "There's been no word yet of any other fatalities, any serious injuries or substantial damage. But we should prepare ourselves to hear of more." It had killed Miles and knocked out power and communications. So it seemed likely the quake had caused further devastation, even if they hadn't heard what that was yet, or who else might've been taken.

Still no one was speaking up to comment or ask questions. Probably they were saving such for when they could get her, or one of the other councilors, on their own, to badger them or demand answers when it would be harder to avoid a direct response.

"Now, until communications are restored, people needing medical treatment will have to rely on a neighbor or person passing by to help. But this is a kind, generous community, and I'm sure many have already stepped into the breach to assist their fellow citizens out there.

"Also, if any of the nodes which receive wireless electricity were damaged in the quake, power being restored may have sparked fires in those locations." She closed her eyes briefly. "Sensors will detect any such problem, but while the net's down those alerts won't go out, so we have to hope that anywhere fire has broken out someone has noticed and is fighting it. Every structure in the compound—even down to the tiniest shack or hut—has one or more handheld extinguishers. And the larger buildings all have fire suppression systems installed. While a node short-circuiting may cause power to fail in isolated places and possibly prevent those systems from activating automatically, they can be engaged manually to put out any fires." And the instructions on how to do it could be accessed on their pads, which would really be useful once the network was back up.

That thought led to her next comment. "Hopefully communications will be restored shortly. And when that happens the FURCSnet will send instant alerts about any urgent problems to particular people. Those who need to know." She hoped they had programmed that properly. "And people in distress will want to call for help. So, while I know you'll all want to contact friends and family and business associates immediately to find out how they are, what the situation is in different areas of the community, I'm asking you to limit those communications as far as possible, to keep the system from being strained, so people with emergencies will be able to get ahold of help."

And as soon as the net was back up, she needed to call Verity, or Ben, to see if one of them could set up a way for the computer to prioritize certain communications. "Thank you for your cooperation."

As she stepped down from the platform, muted beeping came from several pads simultaneously and her own flashed on and off in her purse. Verity had finally restored communications and the alerts were going out.

Now they would find out how bad the situation actually was and the real work would begin, but before she could check to see her own messages, those citizens who hadn't received any alerts—or who had already dealt with them—started their approach.

12:05 a.m. Saturday, May 28th
The main hall of Community Hall

ALVIN FOX WATCHED Caroline skillfully deal with yet another complaining citizen, one of the few who weren't still glued to their pads, and continued considering the new political situation. The demise of the director changed all his calculations. The new widow would garner considerable sympathy as people learned of her husband's death, and the woman wouldn't hesitate to use that. Any attempt to lessen her influence had suddenly become much more difficult. And if he were seen to be undermining her in any way...

The new reality required him to be her staunch supporter for the foreseeable future, but he knew he could use that too. Working *with* her would simply be another way to show his own capacity for leadership. After all, her act necessitated that she be seen to need support, and he would receive considerable approbation if he fulfilled that role. It would tie his political fortune more closely to hers, which looked like a good move at the moment.

Another way the director's death created an opportunity for Alvin—he'd always been quite attracted to Caroline and enjoyed their barbed banter, but she'd always firmly resisted even any hint of a dalliance with him. Now, though, after a suitable period of mourning for her husband...

During the difficult days which were sure to follow, Alvin would be a constant stay for Caroline, in a completely proper way. In public. He could start to court her privately much sooner. And eventually he could take Jonathan Miles' place, not only as director but as her husband as well.

She would prove a valuable asset. Caroline understood people and, more importantly, they sensed that. It created an emotional bond between her and the community. She used that connection to match their irrational feelings and steer their responses in a more helpful direction. With his keen insight and logical mind, he could guide her—and together they would lead the world in the way it should go.

Right now that meant rallying everyone to help recover from the current disaster.

Chapter 22

Sorting Things Out

12:10 a.m. Saturday, May 28th
The second floor of Security HQ

ANTHONY STARED AROUND at all the mess the suppression foam had made of his quarters here at Security and sighed. Much worse than across the hall in the Resource Room, where Ben had made an effort to cover the electronic equipment, but Anthony rarely used these rooms anymore. They'd proved convenient to keep changes of clothes. And he liked taking a shower here so he looked nice and felt fresh when he went home. But they wouldn't be so handy anymore, not for a while.

The important thing, though, was that the whole first floor remained relatively unscathed. Hope had quickly covered the desk and other furniture downstairs, in his office and the conference room and the break room. The lobby was designed for easy cleaning. And with the net back up he'd been able to see the data from the sensors, which confirmed the fire had been completely extinguished.

So, they could continue to run everything out of HQ. But until the damaged node could be replaced, the building was without power and the doors could not be secured. Or the three cells meant for detaining people temporarily, which also would have been handy to have available at the moment, to solve one of the several thorny problems Security was dealing with. Because the detention center had been evacuated and would be unsuitable for use for an extended period of time.

That was one. At least Lisa had shown up there in time to prevent the entire building from burning down. And Greg's injuries were minor enough that he could continue working—as long as he took care. Michelle's management of the inmates had been excellent, and Anthony decided to greenlight her plan for what to do with the prisoners who had behaved. After he'd already paroled Sara, it only made sense. So he looked down at his pad and sent a message to Lisa, telling her to go ahead and organize those seventeen inmates into workgroups.

They couldn't be kept out in the Yard indefinitely, and if they helped out—clearing debris, cleaning up, and such—their sentences would be commuted. But if they caused trouble...

Anthony turned and stepped back into the hall, repressing a sigh as he started down the stairs.

Extended incarceration as a threat had become problematic for now, but presumably they would fix that, and there was always expulsion. Maybe David would get his way and the council would send away the worst troublemakers. Put them out of the compound. That would make more work for the guards anyway, to keep them from sneaking back in. Well, based on Michelle's report, most detainees were eager to show they could contribute to the community if it would earn them back their freedom.

As for the hard cases, he'd arranged for the four Sara had incapacitated to be transported over to the clinic for treatment. David and Susan were driving one of the large carts over to the detention center at that moment to pick them up, and those two should be able to handle them.

He'd sent Sara to the detention center too. She could bring Hennessey here, as well as the padlocks they'd been using to secure some of the cells there—only, when the others were returned from the clinic after receiving medical attention, that would be five prisoners to hold here in three cells. He would have to put Marigold in one, the men would have to double up. Not a long-term solution.

Anthony sighed. That still left Brandon Radley, out there somewhere and on the loose, intending to cause trouble. The question was what kind of trouble, and where.

Reaching the ground floor, Anthony found Ben pacing back and forth in the corridor, trying to look alert. And appearing disconsolate. "You did good." He'd put the fire out before it did much damage and couldn't be expected to stop someone like Radley on his own. "And you still think Brandon was trying to get into the gun safe?"

Ben halted where he was and frowned. "It's the only thing that makes sense, sir. He didn't hurt me or Hope much, so he hadn't come for revenge. And there's nothing else in the Resource Room he would have found much use for."

As soon as he'd heard Ben's report, he had sent Kat a message, warning her Brandon might head to the Guard HQ, hoping to find the weapons there he had failed to get his hands on here. That might still be his goal, and he'd know there were guns there.

On the other hand, there were other places firearms could be found in the compound even if not as easily, and Brandon might have abandoned the idea of getting a gun. After all, there were plenty of other weapons lying around all over.

As for where he might go, aside from the Guard headquarters—which would not be a brilliant move on the man's part, but then he'd never been bright—he held a lot of grudges against a lot of people. Sara and Anthony had visited the Radley home immediately after leaving the detention center. Wondering if Brandon had headed there. Though whether that would have been for refuge or revenge remained an open question. But he hadn't been there.

Well, they'd warned George and Martha. If the couple decided to shelter their son rather than turn him in, at least he wouldn't be out in the compound causing mischief.

After that, Anthony and Sara had headed to the Rec Center. Radley and his reprobate friends spent lots of time there—back before they'd been caught—and fugitives often returned to familiar haunts. The massive building had been dark and empty with the people who'd been inside milling about and looking lost outside in the aftermath of the quake.

The lights had come back on while Anthony and Sara were still searching the evacuated building and made things more difficult. Power returning somehow prompted a lot of people to come back into the Rec Center. And the crowds had hampered hunting for a single individual.

At least once the network was online again, Anthony had been able to send out an alert—everyone was warned about Radley now, and some observant citizen might see him and call it in. He had to hope no one would do anything more than that, that they would let Security do its job. Because Brandon was a dangerous man.

Really, Anthony ought to be out there searching for him rather than twiddling his thumbs here. But under the circumstances, he couldn't leave Ben and Hope on their own again—he'd have to wait to leave until Kirkland came back, and the man was *walking* here from the Green. Moseying, more like.

Once his deputy had returned, though, Anthony could rendezvous with Sara and resume hunting for Radley. In spite of having worked all day—and from what he'd heard having had quite a rough evening—Lisa had volunteered to help Michelle and Greg supervise the prisoner work detail.

David would be of more use working for Security than the Guards, so once he and Susan had delivered the treated prisoners back here from the clinic, Anthony would send them out on patrol. And after Salazar and Gabe had *walked* to the clinic to retrieve their cart, they could resume their regular patrol. It would mean two pairs of officers to respond to calls across the fourteen square-mile compound. Which wouldn't be enough.

Everyone else would have to pitch in too, and it would help to have power restored here at HQ.

12:15 a.m. Saturday, May 28th
North of the Green

SARA STRODE ALONG the empty walkway toward the detention center, having left behind all the areas now swarming with activity—people checking on friends, family, and property, cleaning up where they could and catching up with what had happened elsewhere while they worked. She had sensed their relief at the return of lights and the net in how they kept checking their pads. That made her even more eager to retrieve her own.

The main reason for Chief Nelson sending Sara back to the prison was to take custody of the traitor Hennessey, who had escaped then been recaptured, who had been returned to the detention center, and who now needed to be transferred over to HQ. She didn't mind acting as a delivery person or a babysitter. It was far better than being behind bars. Only, she thought she'd be more useful hunting, or rather continuing to hunt, for Brandon Radley, who represented an active threat to the community.

But then, that was what she would've been considered herself, if she'd escaped rather than staying and trying to help. And she trusted the chief. He'd make the right decisions, make the best use of what assets he had to deal with the myriad problems they faced. So if he wanted her to take this detour to the detention center, she wasn't complaining. Besides, it would give her the opportunity to pick up her pad —they kept the prisoners' pads in the staff area, and only let them use the devices during specified times —presuming it hadn't been damaged in the fire.

She sincerely prayed it still worked. Being able to receive alerts, to communicate with the chief and other officers was the only way she'd be effective as a 'trainee on special probation'. That was what Nelson now called her, and she needed to do a good job if she was going to get her life back on track. Allowing her to go off on her own like this, even on a routine errand, was a precious measure of trust. Which showed she was off to a good start.

They'd had to separate some to search the Recreation Center effectively, and she'd been surprised he gave her that much latitude. Then when the network came back online, he had sent her off alone to take care of Hennessey. Trusting Sara to move him meant the chief really was giving her a chance. Perhaps if she proved herself with this...

When they returned to hunting for Radley, they could search more ground splitting up, and he knew she'd be capable of taking down the fugitive by herself. What he might not be sure of was whether she could do that without using excessive force, the obstacle that had kept her a trainee in the past.

She wasn't sure herself if she could get past the issue. Because she wasn't sure why she had a problem going overboard in the first place. Even so, she would have to rein in that tendency. Whatever that took.

Suddenly she was being tackled to the ground—somebody collided with her legs from the left side to send her flying off the walkway and sprawling to the grass. Before she could even begin to react, she felt her arm being twisted behind her, levering her face into the lawn as a knee pressed against the small of her back. By then she knew who it was had brought her down and pinned her to the ground and offered no resistance.

"I suppose you want revenge. For your mom. I can't say I blame you." The side of her mouth being squashed distorted her voice, but she thought those words sounded clear enough. To be understood, or so she hoped.

"I tackled you because you've escaped from the detention center." Kat shifted slightly. "But I don't have any zip-ties on me, and I don't have time to sit around waiting for someone to come pick you up, so I'll have to frog-march you back to your cell."

Sara sighed. "By all means, take me back to the detention center. It's where I was headed anyway—do you think I'd be going there if I'd escaped?" She let her muscles relax. "Better yet, call your husband

and ask *him* what I'm doing. The chief should have told you anyway—you have a right to know—though maybe he was afraid to say."

"What are you talking about?"

Fighting back a second sigh, Sara tried to move her head so she could catch Kat's eye. "The disaster has Security stretched thin, and Chief Nelson chose to parole me so I could help. A couple prisoners *did* escape, and he wanted my assistance hunting down those fugitives."

"Tony texted to warn me Brandon Radley could be headed for Guard HQ to get his grubby hands on some guns." Kat snorted, but it didn't sound meant for Sara.

"Lisa Courdray ran across Hennessey, took him into custody and back to the detention center. They had to evacuate everybody out of the building there, and now the chief wants the worst offenders moved into the cells at Security."

Kat still hadn't eased up on Sara's arm. "You're supposed to transfer all those dangerous prisoners, are you? By yourself?"

Sara twisted her neck further and finally locked eyes with the other woman. "No, four are headed to the hospital. I'm only meant to move Hennessey to HQ. Then I suppose I'll see what the boss wants me to do next." She sighed. "Look, you have good reasons not to trust me—"

"You betrayed your position, the job, the whole community. You were going to murder my mother. There's no question of trust."

She was going to get a bad crick in her neck but deserved worse than that. "I don't think I would've killed her—that wasn't the plan, and I didn't intend to—but I was so messed up back then, I'm not sure. I can't really say what I might've done."

Kat grunted. "Are you blaming the Gravity Bug for your behavior, then?"

"Whether it was that or just being a jerk doesn't matter. My judgment was horrible. I'm grateful to you for stopping me before I did something worse." Sara turned her face back to the grass. "It took me a while to learn that lesson. To be thankful that I was turned from the path I was on, and you did me that favor." She forced back the threatening tears. "But I understand why you can't forgive me." She'd had a hard time coming to the place where she was able to accept forgiveness, she didn't expect Kat to grant it.

She felt the other woman shift, then sensed her pull out a pad with her free hand and heard her tap something. Then Kat's voice. Simply, "Sara King?" Whoever Kat had called—Chief Nelson?—answered at some length. "Right. Understood."

Suddenly released from the hold, Sara took her time rolling over onto her back and working out the stiffness in her arm, her neck. All while attempting to read the expression in Kat's eyes. Whatever that look was, though, it was undecipherable.

"You'd better get on your feet and get a move on if you don't want to get in trouble again. Chief Nelson's a good boss, but he can't abide a slacker. And you're on thin ice to begin with." Kat turned, began walking away. "But I'm hoping you make it." Then the woman was running.

Sara stood and watched her for a long moment, then took off herself, sprinting toward the detention center. Her emotions were in turmoil. But that was no excuse for not getting on with the job.

Chapter 23

Determining Priorities

12:35 a.m. Saturday, May 28th
The Community Council Conference Room

PAUL LEANED BACK and scrolled through the latest information on his pad as he waited for Caroline to gavel the Council back into session. The vast majority of public alerts had disappeared. To be replaced by scores of mostly citizen reports—pleas for assistance with various problems and details of how other difficulties had been dealt with. They created an impression, but there was no overview of the situation. This meeting was meant to correct that.

Looking up as Verity finally walked wearily into the chamber—she seemed far more exhausted than he would've expected, but then Paul hadn't seen the deputy director since she'd left him in Admin about two and a half hours ago—he sat up straight and began paying attention. They should start soon.

While he'd been helping get the power back on, apparently Verity had been working to get communications restored. From the look of her, she'd also been putting out a bunch of fires, probably the metaphorical sort rather than the literal, but maybe she had been fighting the real thing as well. She clearly hadn't gotten any rest, had reportedly been too busy to come to the Hall before now.

When Caroline had told them of Director Miles' demise, Paul had assumed Verity would be stepping into that position as his deputy. Turned out, things weren't so simple or straightforward. After the last session had ended, Alvin Fox had approached Paul, made some 'offhand' comments about it.

"Ms. Belue has run the administration quite capably all this time, so it seems best to have her continue in her current role," the man had stated. "But the new director should be someone the community already sees as a leader."

The essence, as Paul eventually gathered, was a plan to change the charter to require the director be one of the councilors, and Alvin Fox had gone as far as suggesting himself for the position. Claiming he was the best qualified.

Though he hadn't said so, Paul had reservations about the idea itself—he hadn't even started to consider who might be a good candidate—the most important being who would really be in charge then.

As it was, Caroline might be called 'first among equals', but she led the council. Paul and the others had a voice in things, and a vote, and they all argued a lot over various decisions. But the First Councilor set the agenda, directed the discussions, and was in effective control of the community. Should another councilor be chosen as director of the FURC institution itself, who would actually lead the council?

Unless they chose Caroline to fill both positions —and that would never happen, no matter the level of her approval or popularity—having two people in charge of the compound competing to influence the seven-member council seemed like a recipe for disaster. And they already had one on their hands.

Not that Paul had any ideas on how to handle it himself, but whenever there had been a question of whether Miles or Caroline had authority over a particular area, the couple had settled the issue with no apparent problems. Behind closed doors. Paul had no desire to know what went on between them, and as long as everything had gone smoothly, he wasn't going to complain. But now, everything would have to change.

And unless he had a brainwave, Paul would listen to everyone else's ideas and just vote for whichever made the most sense. Hopefully one would.

Then Caroline stood and coughed as Verity took her seat at the conference table. “The council is now back in session. Before we hear your individual reports, I just want to say—since the net is online and a lot of citizens may be watching live—I’m so proud of our community. Many of you kept your heads as the quake hit, helped the people in need around you and worked quickly to limit the damage. Thank you all.”

Immediately after she finished, Alvin chimed in with his thanks. “Yes, congratulations everybody. I particularly want to praise the Ag workers, who did not waste any time, I hear, getting to the livestock to take care of the animals, then immediately began to repair the fish tanks and hydroponic pods. Also, we owe a special thanks to Deputy Director Belue, who personally fixed the communications relay, to bring the network back online.”

The man hadn’t mentioned the brave efforts by security officers to deal with a number of crises, and Paul considered thanking them himself even though he still worked for Security—at least part-time, anyway—but before he could decide to speak up, Caroline continued. “Deputy Director Belue will now report on our overall situation. With help from some of you who can add important details about various matters. You may proceed, Verity.” Waving toward the other woman, she resumed her seat.

After quickly consulting her pad, Verity leaned forward and addressed the Chair. "Yes. Before I go into the details of our response to this emergency, I need to describe what we know so far about the nature of the disaster itself. Of course, we don't really have earthquakes in Florida, or haven't before this." She looked across the table at Paul and nodded, apparently asking him to elaborate.

He cleared his throat. "On those rare occasions we've felt tremors here in the past, they've been the result of quakes far out in the Gulf or in states north of us. Florida doesn't have any major faults."

Somebody sighed, though Paul didn't see who—and Alvin made a rolling motion with his hand suggesting they move things along. Paul gave the floor back to Verity.

She squinted at Fox, then continued. "And several witnesses have reported seeing a streak of light in the sky—an apparent meteor strike—five minutes or so before feeling the shaking start. That approximate timing, added to the very limited seismological data we have access to, has helped our researchers estimate the epicenter of the quake." Again she nodded at Paul to explain.

He gestured with his pad. "The report with the technical details has been posted for anybody who'd like to review them, but the gist is this—the experts believe that at about nine thirty-nine this evening a meteorite crashed off the northeast coast of the US. Without more data, they can't pinpoint a precise location. Or estimate the size of the object that struck the earth. But—"

Alvin interrupted. "You're saying this meteorite strike actually caused the quake?"

"What we felt wasn't the traditional earthquake caused by shifting plates, but an impact quake. And yes, the explosive force of the impact created a seismic wave that rippled through the earth's crust and caused the upheaval we experienced here."

Tracy gasped. "That must have been a massive meteor."

Paul nodded. "Based on the intensity we measured here—the energy of the wave would have dissipated the farther it traveled—they were able to estimate the explosive power of the impact. That would have been a product of the mass of the object and the speed it was moving at when it struck. But it would have to have been huge."

Into the silence following that statement, Verity spoke. "The important thing for people to know is—because of the nature of the quake, they don't think there will be any aftershocks. So we can go forward focused on repairs and recovery operations without worrying about further disaster."

Caroline looked to her, then Paul. "What about the possibility of a tsunami?"

Verity nodded, then shook her head and looked again to Paul. “Yes, but it doesn’t concern us. Such a huge object would’ve displaced a massive amount of water. And if the impact was as close to the coast as we believe, it probably caused a surge that would swamp the shore up there. Also, yes—the upheaval to the ocean floor caused by the explosive force—as it hit the coastal shelf rather than the deep—should have created a tsunami.”

More gasps, but he continued. “However, while we would expect to see those waves reach the Florida coastline, even the largest tsunami would be unlikely to make it more than ten miles inland.”

Thankfully Verity took up the baton. “So, while there is probably massive flooding up and down the Atlantic coast, even as far as the Keys, the FURC itself shouldn’t experience any.” Sighs of relief came when they heard that, and she switched the subject. “Now, though Dr. Harker is understandably unable to attend, she’s asked her fellow councilor—and her friend—Dean Tracy Johnson to present her update. Professor Johnson?”

Tracy smiled nervously around the table. “Casualties are currently receiving treatment at the clinic, which sustained little damage, and while staffing was a problem initially, they now have enough personnel available to handle their patient load. However, the ambulances remain trapped in the bay and cannot respond to emergency calls. They're relying on those requiring help to reach the medical center under their own power or be brought there by good samaritans. And they're asking for anyone who has construction experience and the proper tools to see if they can come repair those ambulance bay doors. As soon as possible."

She paused and glanced down at her pad before continuing. "So far there are six reported fatalities. And over four dozen debilitated or seriously injured citizens. The sisters are asking for volunteers to donate blood, assuming they can make it to the medical center."

Verity thanked the woman, then continued with her own report. "As you all know, some of the electricity reception nodes were damaged in the quake, and when power was restored it started some small fires. But I'm glad to report those have all been extinguished. Several people are suffering from some smoke inhalation, and a few received minor burns, but there were no serious injuries. As a result of the fires. Unfortunately, several buildings are currently without power."

Paul started scanning through that report as he listened. Security HQ was one of those in the dark.

"They'll need new nodes installed. And in some cases repairs to the electrical wiring as well." Verity looked to Jeffrey, who shrugged. Leaning back, the landscaper addressed the ceiling. "That's a top priority, of course, for the buildings that are otherwise still usable."

He glanced around at his fellow councilors, then turned his gaze upward again. "I'm sorry to inform everyone that Cameron's Luxury Suites burnt to the ground. As well as several warehouses in the area—most of them empty, thankfully. A few other buildings will require extensive renovations before being usable again. Including the detention center."

Verity interrupted. "Related to that, I also need to let everyone know that while the worst offenders are still being detained, most were paroled—to help with the cleanup."

Giving her a curt nod, Jeffrey continued. "We'll have to wait for daylight to fully assess what repairs other buildings will require. I'm sure you've all noticed the cracks in some of the walls, and we'll have to inspect foundations carefully. But most can continue to be used safely, for the time being."

Alvin interjected. "Especially if there aren't going to be any aftershocks."

"Exactly. A more pressing need, come daylight, will be repairing the roads and walkways. With the power on and light to see, the breaks in those aren't terribly dangerous. If people are careful." His tone sounded skeptical. "But we have a lot of work to do over the next several weeks—if not months—and we will need to be able to get quickly and easily around the compound." He frowned. "I'm afraid regrading the other areas and repairing the lawns will have to wait."

Caroline nodded. "We've all had a rough night, and I think everything except emergencies can wait until tomorrow—later this morning, I mean—to get moving on. So let's adjourn, try to get at least a few hours' sleep, and start again at daylight."

Verity sighed. "I second the motion."

And Paul stood. "The rest of you, go ahead and go home if you want. Security obviously needs help—and they need it now. So I'm heading over to HQ to see what I can do." After all that experience he'd had earlier this evening, he could probably even replace their power node. He'd have to check the wiring first, though, and make sure the regular circuits could handle the load.

Not waiting for the formal vote to close the session, he strode out of the conference room using his clearance as a councilor to pull up the schematic for Security headquarters and began reviewing the wiring diagram and mentally making a list of supplies, which he'd have to get at the electrical labs. Thankfully he had a cart and could zip right over, collect a tech or two, and be back at HQ soon.

Chapter 24

Keeping Busy

12:50 a.m. Saturday, May 28th
The FURC main thoroughfare

KAT'S THOUGHTS TUMBLED as she jogged, the same thoughts spinning through her brain over and over again, like laundry cycling in a dryer. Not light and fluffy clothes, though. More like shoes, or something heavy and clunky anyway, thumping and banging against the boundaries of her mind.

Her dad was dead. As soon as communications had been restored, before she'd even left Tim at the back gate, Caroline had called to tell her that. Kat's mother had been too busy to talk long—no surprise there—but what else was there to say. Words would be a shabby bandage for that wound. And Kat kept it open, wanted it raw and exposed and hurting, because she felt it should. For all the good times she'd shared with her father growing up, she hadn't made much time for him as an adult.

Ken was alive. But her bear of a boss might not walk again—or if he did, it sounded unlikely he'd be able to get around as gracefully as he used to. As he should, and would expect to. That could crush even someone as tough as Chief Cameron. Or maybe especially a person so robust.

She'd have to take over for him with the Guards for the foreseeable future, which would just rub salt in the wounds—hers and his. At least it would help her keep busy.

Dealing with the rest of the aftermath from this night's disaster would insure that. But those things—Wagner's death, the injured guards, the damaged fence and wall and buildings—none of that pounded against her heart. Rather, she found them welcome distractions.

Like trying to think where Brandon Radley was and what he'd be up to, and whether she'd have the opportunity to capture him. If he thought he might be able to get a gun at the Guard HQ, he was a moron. Of course, she knew he was. So the man might show up so she could take him down.

But power had already been restored when he'd been seen at Security, so by the time he could reach the Guards' armory the room would've been secure, and all the rifles and handguns in there were always kept inside locked cabinets. Kat kept her own sniper rifle in a gun safe in her office. And the chief did keep his sidearm in a safe as well—at least when he wasn't wearing it, and he almost always was.

Of course, with Ken being badly injured and the flurry of activity which must have accompanied getting him over to the clinic, what had become of that gun he would've been wearing? David and the other guards were well trained in firearm safety, so she had to believe they'd have thought of that. But after all, she didn't *know* and couldn't be sure.

On the other hand, Brandon would have no way to know about that potential opportunity, and could well have considered the difficulty of obtaining one of the guns at the Guard HQ. But if so, where would he go?

Suddenly it hit her, and she swerved, ran up off the road and across the sidewalk and onto the grass stretching between buildings. Uneven ground, broken and treacherous for unwary feet. But there was plenty of light and her senses were sharp. She could see the tall, single-story square of headquarters, her previous destination, in the distance. Curving away to her right as she angled further to her left.

If Radley were clever—and bad guys often had a natural instinct that could resemble cleverness—he might think of trying to ambush an armed guard as they went in or out of HQ, to steal a weapon from a man who already had one. Of course, guards usually traveled at least in pairs, if not even larger groups when on duty, and off duty didn't go around armed. But if Brandon were prepared to be patient, eventually he might find a lone guard with a gun.

If he had *that* idea, though, it might occur to him to check the barracks. With all hands on deck, none of the men were likely to be there, but they each had a rifle stored away by their bunks in case of needing to muster in a minute. Those should be secured also, but under the circumstances...

Regardless, an on-duty guard sometimes had to run back to the barracks for one reason or another—and carried their weapon when they went. Unlikely that Radley would think of that, as he hadn't been a guard himself. But he had hung out with one who'd turned traitor.

If nothing else, she could check to make sure no one had left a rifle lying around unsecured, and take a look around the area to see if someone was skulking about.

The barracks had no windows, but then nobody spent much time there except to sleep. Kat was glad to find the door locked. Using her pad to unlock the entrance electronically, she pushed it open from the side, and swiftly scanned the bright interior space—of what had seemed a dark building—from the relatively dim outdoors. And saw nobody, and nothing untoward.

Slipping inside, she turned and looked in all the corners she couldn't see from outside and found the main room really was bare. No guards, but she had not expected to find any, and no Radley, which also wasn't a surprise since the door had been locked.

More importantly, no weapons in sight. Nevertheless, she crossed the wide space and searched all the smaller rooms at the back of the building. Then returned to the front and double-checked that every locker was secure. No problems here.

Now she just needed to send a general message to all the guards—on and off duty—warning them to stick together and be alert for a possible ambush.

She'd started typing into her pad as she left the barracks, but raised her head when she heard some soft footfalls in the distance. A lone guard, with his rifle slung over his shoulder, heading her way. Just what she wanted to warn them about.

Recognizing Alvarez—he must've already delivered the injured Hodges into somebody else's care—she sighed. He had to have come out the back door from headquarters, and hopefully he'd been watching as he exited to make sure no one slipped inside. Regardless, she'd have to dress him down. Though he'd had a rough shift and was no doubt exhausted, and wouldn't get more than a short break under the circumstances, that couldn't be used as an excuse to avoid proper vigilance. Other people's lives were at stake, as well as the man's own.

She was wondering what would be the best way to dress him down without making him feel too bad when a silhouette moved swiftly out of the shadows toward Alvarez. Sprinting forward, she held back a shout—it might only distract him, turn his attention in the wrong direction.

As the attacker came into the light, it was Brandon. She assumed he was attempting to be stealthy in his approach, but he still made much more noise than Kat did running full pelt. Radley didn't appear to have noticed her yet, but at least Alvarez seemed to have sensed the man coming at him. Turned just a bit too late.

He was bringing his gun up between them when Brandon collided with him and took a solid hit, and lurched backward from the impact. But managed to stay on his feet. Both men now had hold of the rifle and struggled for possession.

Then Kat was there, shouting to get their attention—Radley used the distraction to wrench the gun away from Alvarez, but failed to pivot in time to use it. She kicked his leg out from under him and spun as he tottered, grabbing the rifle. And slammed the butt of the gun across his temple. He collapsed into an unconscious heap.

Kat handed the rifle back to Alvarez, then shook her head. “He’ll be dead weight now. Help me haul him into the brig”—she could call Security and have them come pick him up at their leisure—“and then I won’t reprimand you for being sloppy.”

The guard grunted, but slung the rifle back over his shoulder and squatted to grab one of Brandon’s arms. Between them they lifted him enough to drag him back to HQ without too much trouble. Tossing him onto the cot in the cell, Kat sighed and thanked Alvarez. “Now go back to the barracks, secure your gun, and get some rest. I’ll sign you out through six in the morning.”

Raising one eyebrow—and the left corner of his mouth—the guard seemed surprised. “I ought to be the one thanking you, Lieutenant. I expected I’d be working the whole night through.”

She smiled wide. “We’ve got plenty of guys who are fresh on the gates for now—but they will have to be relieved in the morning. So sleep now. I’m sure tomorrow will be tough too.”

Letting him leave, Kat strode down the corridor to the Chief’s office, where she discovered Sgt. Carruthers squaring things away. He rose from putting something in a filing cabinet and turned to give her a crisp salute. Talk about ingrained habits.

“At ease, Sergeant. You’re not in the army anymore, remember.” Over five years out of the service and more than five working for the FURC and these veterans acted as if they were still in the military. "I was never in the armed services, as you well know." Yet as soon as she'd been put in a position above them they'd started saluting.

"Whatever you say, Lieutenant." What she had said before, and repeatedly, but never took. "You'll be taking over here, then?"

Kat hesitated. The last report had the chief still in surgery and likely out of it through the night, and until Ken was awake, alert, and compos mentis, she was in command. That didn't mean she would have to sit around the office on her duff, though. Things were too quiet here.

Probably she should send Sgt. Carruthers to the front gate to take charge from Lacey Petrovich. But the former Russian merc could use this experience, get the other guards used to taking her orders. And Kat didn't want to be alone with her thoughts.

So she shook her head. "You've been doing fine here, Sergeant. I'll let you keep holding the fort for now, while I take care of some urgent business." He was too disciplined to ask, but she saw the question in his eyes. "The wild predators out there—animals, but not the human variety—are our major danger at the moment." She wanted to protect her guards, at the same time she'd prefer they didn't have to shoot any more of the poor creatures.

Carruthers nodded. "You've seen the reports, I know. Guards have already killed two of those feral hogs in self-defense."

"And I almost had to kill a panther trying to get over a downed section of fence." The thought of an animal getting caught in the concertina wire forced a shudder. "We'd have an even worse problem if any got into the compound proper. We may have a way to prevent that, though."

She reminded the sergeant about the sonic post fencing system the techs had been working on. The ultrasonic noise was pretty well proven to repel lots of animals, but they'd been trying to fine tune it—to keep away Gravity Bug infected humans as well. An obvious tactic, as it could give normal people headaches with extended exposure. And this would be a good time to test the technology.

"That sounds like a good plan, Lieutenant. How about I detail off a pair of guards to go get the posts and circle the compound planting them?"

Kat shook her head. "They're all needed to keep the gates defended. I'll take care of this myself. It's a little dangerous."

The sergeant squinted. "Which is why you'd do best to take at least one with you to watch your back if nothing else."

Kat shook her head. "I'll move faster, easier, if I don't have to worry about a partner." It'd be different if she could take Tony with her, but that was not an option at the moment. “Any carts available?”

Carruthers lifted both eyebrows. “You’re going to drive around outside the compound?”

“No, sergeant. Just over to the electronic labs—to pick up those posts.” After she saw how big those were, and how heavy, she could decide the best way to carry them, but she always felt lighter on her own two feet. And freer, no matter what she was encumbered with.

“Yes, mam. The large cart is gone, but the small cart is still out in the side lot.”

Kat nodded. “Then I’ll let you carry on, and get on with my own business.” And if she drove fast on the cracked walkways, the hyperfocus that required would keep her from thinking of other things.

Chapter 25

Powerful Surges

5:35 a.m. Saturday, May 28th
The second floor of the Medical Center

AMITA STARED INTO the mirror and saw dark bags under her eyes. No wonder, considering what last night had been like, but maybe she should use a little concealer. She knew she was no great beauty—attractive enough, plenty of proof for that, though if she'd make more of an effort...

Sighing, she set her purse on the washstand and dug until she found the small makeup kit she hardly every used. Since her senior year in high school and the decision to become a doctor, she'd set aside any idea of intentionally trying to attract men, who distracted her too much as it was. She'd concentrated on her career instead, and been richly rewarded.

But for over three years now, since she first met David, Amita had actively sought a relationship and been frustrated by how difficult it had been, in part because her pride wouldn't allow her to change herself. Alright, sometimes she'd made a little effort to 'pretty herself up'—as her mother had put it—to get him to pursue her. But it hadn't been enough.

She could see he was attracted to her even when she didn't make a special effort, but still she needed to lead him every step of the way. Only it was more like dragging a stubborn mule.

The man had too much self-control, and she refused to literally throw herself at him. So, more than three years of subtle suggestions and indirect flirtation—sometimes becoming pretty blatant about it—hadn't gotten her very far. All the more frustrating, she found, because he clearly cared for her.

David enjoyed spending as much time together with her as their schedules allowed and would even go out on 'dates'—but Amita always had to push him a little. He would at least visit her without prompting. If she didn't suggest something, however, he'd happily sit in her living room just talking. Or sitting in silent contentment. Holding her in his arms and simply relaxing at the end of a hard day—which she appreciated. But he took it no further on his own.

And if Amita had occasionally felt brazen to the point of kissing him, he responded warmly enough, but never with the consuming passion she hoped to kindle. Perhaps he didn't have that in him.

Looking at the finished result in the mirror, she nodded to herself in satisfaction and started to pull her hair back into the usual ponytail. Then, instead, she shoved the scrunchie back in her purse, leaving her hair loose around her shoulders. Better. Especially this morning.

Last night, more than exhausted, she'd crawled into one of the many empty beds in the unused second-floor wards and pretty much passed out. Only a few hours of sleep had intervened before her unsettled mind had woken her while it was still dark outside. The death and destruction she'd seen had impacted her more than her conscious mind wanted to admit. Her subconscious called her a coward.

For all the improvements generated by their altered DNA and the fact that her biological clock had slowed to a virtual standstill, life was short, and the future was uncertain. While she wasn't *un*happy, it didn't feel like she was living life to the fullest. Was her pride preventing her from seizing the joy which could be hers?

Walking back out onto the ward, she saw David sitting up on the bed beside the one she had slept on —Amita had awakened to find him asleep there just a few minutes ago—rubbing a hand across his eyes, running the other through his hair. Adorable.

He smiled as she approached. "You look rested and refreshed."

Well, 'beautiful' would've been better, but she'd take what she could get. "Did *you* rest well?"

Nodding, David slid off the sheets and stretched his arms wide with a yawn. "I was told I'd be needed more in the morning, so I came up not long after you. Went straight to sleep without any trouble."

"Which means you only got three hours at best. And they'll probably work you hard today."

He just grinned. "No doubt they will. But while last night was rough and today will be tougher, this will still be a walk in the park compared to what I've been through before." She lifted a skeptical eyebrow at him. "Alright, not quite a walk in the park. But I can handle hard work."

Pursing her lips, she wondered again if he had a passionate nature or not. Perhaps he was only old-fashioned. In which case, the bold step she planned to take might scare him off, but she was committed to making this move. If it didn't work, Amita could at least finally give up on an impossible dream. If it did, maybe she'd find out how much heat there was in him.

"David, will you marry me?"

He gaped at her, which wasn't the most gratifying response. Or very promising. "You want me for a husband?"

Nodding, she wondered why he seemed to have trouble accepting the idea. Was the age difference a problem for him, that she was thirteen years older? Or did he not have sufficient self-confidence, would not credit her wanting him as a husband rather than something less than that? "I want to spend the rest of my life with you." More than that, but she didn't want to spook him.

He shook his head slowly. "I don't think I could make you happy."

For someone so smart, he could really be dense sometimes. But it might be best not to say that now —she could criticize him later, after they were married. Or after he turned her down. "Trust me, marrying you would make me happy. Well?"

Taking her hands in his—too bad he didn't take a knee, but she shouldn't be greedy—he smiled and bent his head to give her a chaste kiss. "I should be the one asking you. Of course I'd be thrilled to have you for my wife, for the rest of my life. If you'll consent to settling for me?"

"Oh, David, don't be a fool. I said I want you. I meant it."

Then his hands fell to her hips and he pulled her closer. Much closer. And this time there was nothing friendly about the way he kissed her.

Chapter 25

7:35 a.m. Saturday, May 28th
In the southeast section of the compound

DAVID STAYED ALERT as he broke up the last of the walkway he'd marked off. Though he needed to be careful with the electric jackhammer—while it was less powerful than the gas-powered, it was still a dangerous tool, if a thankfully quieter one. Though he needed to watch his back—the work crew he was supervising consisted of three paroled prisoners. A silly smile was stuck on his face. This morning had left him stunned and amazingly, incredibly happy.

He hadn't wanted to leave Amita for anything—the work waiting for him appealing even less than it had before—but an even more important job waited for her. They both had their duty to do, and after an extended embrace had managed to break apart and go their separate ways. But later today they'd make it official, and tonight they'd be man and wife.

Backing away from the debris, he gestured at it. "Clear the chunks of concrete." There was a wheelbarrow to put it in for recycling—some things could not be improved upon. "Then we'll have to regrade the ground beneath." Really, a single person should be able to do this on their own. At best, it was maybe a two-man job. Over that and more people just got in the way.

But first he had to teach these how to do it, and do the job right, then make sure they could. He had been chosen for this in part because he was trained. Not only in the work itself, but in handling troublemakers as a security officer, and these three needed a firm hand. And in part because he had experience teaching the inexperienced.

Once they'd cleared the debris, he poked a steel pole into the dirt to make sure firmer ground below would still support the walkway, then dug out a bit, shoveled a mix of dirt and small concrete chunks in the sunken hollow—there was a second wheelbarrow filled with earth—and then started packing it down, adding plain dirt and packing it down again. David explained what he was doing each step of the way—to him it was too obvious to need explaining, but he had learned nothing was simple enough to skip.

Stomping the heel of his boot back and forth on the patch of cleared ground between solid sections, he finally felt it had been compressed as firmly as it could. Grabbing the steel rake, he began to demonstrate how to level it off—another crew would follow behind them to fix wooden boundaries and pour the cement, and he had to prepare the ground properly for them—when the men standing around watching him gasped. Even as he looked up, though, the water was lapping at his feet. A wave only a few inches high rolled softly but swiftly over everything.

Stunned, David could only turn his head. Stare at the water sliding across the compound, the roads and the grass and the walkways. He looked down to see it just covered the tops of his boots.

He'd seen flooding before and much worse than this, but he'd never actually witnessed the water appearing so suddenly, with no rain coming down. So where had it come from? While waiting in the hospital last night, he had watched the council sessions and heard that the experts said the FURC was much too far inland to see any effect from a potential tsunami. But what else could this be?

And however little water there was, it was more than an annoyance. All the work they'd done so far this morning would be ruined—the cement they had poured behind him wouldn't set, and they'd have to clear and regrade every section before beginning all over again.

Even as he was thinking that, the waters diminished. Soil and cracks quickly absorbed a lot, but it also rolled backward like a receding wave, leaving a lot of soggy ground behind, and plenty of work to be redone, however brief that flooding had been, and a very bad feeling in the pit of David's stomach. That worse was still to come.

Chapter 26

Hard Realities

10:40 a.m. Saturday, May 28th
Outside the Community Council Conference Room

VERITY BREATHED SLOW and deep, gathering her thoughts before entering. This would be an extremely difficult council session. Of course, every one was, but some more than others, and the report she gave them would certainly be an unpleasant and unwelcome shock. At least for most of them. She'd already apprised Caroline—as the woman was First Councilor, Verity could get away with informing her before the rest—but she hadn't confided these findings in anyone else. Not even Paul, whose feedback might've been interesting. Nor her own son.

Soon everyone would know, though, and everyone could contribute their opinions, but the councilors first of all. They'd have to—or should, anyway—watch what they said. The whole community would pay attention to this session, many viewing live, but all seeing and hearing and analyzing everything before long. Probably people would replay the recording of this meeting multiple times as they attempted to take it in.

Which reminded her that she had to be careful. Her own words would be among those gone over to look for hidden meanings or used as a basis for rank speculation. So she took another minute to concentrate her mind on what she should—and should not—say.

Taking a last lungful of the freer air in the corridor, she marched into the conference room. Taking her seat to the right of Caroline, she placed her pad on the table in front of her and waited. The two had discussed how best to play this. They'd talked about it a lot.

Caroline called the new session to start. "Since Acting Director Belue has now joined us, we should begin. I know you were all expecting this to kick off with status updates on repairs and recovery efforts, but after this morning's flooding, I'm sure everyone would like to hear about that first." She turned and glared at Verity. "Last night you said we didn't have to worry about waves from a tsunami. That nothing would reach us here."

"Last night I provided an early assessment. The best the few experts who could be found could offer based on the limited data we had then. This morning we'd already assembled a fuller team, had them analyzing what happened with more complete data, when the first wave surprised us all." A second and third wave had rolled through after that. Each even smaller than the initial one. "And their conclusions now predict"—with admirable hindsight—"what we experienced earlier today."

She had much more to say, but was interrupted by Councilor Fox. "And what, pray tell, do we know now about the disaster that we didn't last night?"

Verity sighed. "We were able to retrieve a bit of information from one of the still functioning weather satellites and confirm the meteor was larger than initial estimates. Creating a tsunami larger than all those we have records of, one that could reach even this far inland. Thankfully those waves were tiny by the time they got here. And the good news is, there should be no more." According to the experts who'd been wrong before, but she believed they'd gotten it right with that.

Jeffrey Minchin leaned forward. "The question then is, can we proceed with assessing damages and making repairs? Fixing the roads and walkways, as we'd only started to do, will clearly have to wait until the ground's dried out, but as for the rest?"

Verity nodded. “For the most part we can move forward immediately with the reconstruction plans, presuming we want to.”

The perplexed look he gave her was expected as he hadn’t heard the bad news yet. But it took Caroline to ask the obvious. “Why wouldn’t we? The rebuilding should begin as soon as possible.”

“It should, if we choose to proceed with repairs at all.” Verity looked around at the other councilors sitting at the table, all there except Dr. Harker, who had once again been too busy to attend. “I’m afraid the experts have been busy studying the continuing effects of last night’s disaster, and their conclusions are disturbing.”

Caroline fed her the follow-up question. “What do you mean ‘continuing effects’?”

“First, the quake itself caused considerable subsidence—collapsing some of the ground beneath us. Because the bedrock below the state is mostly limestone, which is soluble and porous, Florida has seen a lot of sinkhole activity throughout its history, particularly Central Florida. And the shaking has likely accelerated that. Then, those waves may have been small enough above ground to seem fairly harmless—below the surface, they’ll have eroded a lot of that limestone and pulled the particulates back out when they ebbed, further destabilizing the foundation beneath the peninsula.”

Jeffrey swore and Tracy looked terrified. "Florida's sinking into the ocean?"

Paul appeared thoughtful. "I think she's saying some sizable sinkholes should be expected here and could cause considerable damage to some buildings —far more than the quake did."

Fox squinted hard at her. "That may mean lots more work in the near future, more reconstruction, but that's no reason to avoid making the repairs we can now. Because of further disasters that might or might not happen, and you can't say when?"

Verity stood and pushed her palms at them and waited a moment to make sure they'd stopped talking. "I'll try to address those questions you have already asked. But then please allow me to finish my report so we can have a more informed discussion." She turned to Tracy. "First, the crust supporting us is quite stable, and most of the peninsula is enough above sea level that no one thinks we're in any danger of sinking into the ocean. Not exactly."

Caroline prompted her. "Not exactly?"

"It's complicated, but I'll try to keep this simple for everyone." Verity met Paul's gaze. "Yes, the experts expect increased sinkhole activity throughout the region, but it's more than that. They believe the limestone bedrock has become porous to the point, now, that we'll see continual inflow of ocean waters further softening the ground below. And the waves from the tsunami have oversaturated the soil. They don't expect we *will* dry out. Ever. Most of the state it seems, and some of southern Georgia, will turn to swamp."

There were gasps, but thankfully nobody interrupted—they were sitting there stunned, as she had imagined they would be when they heard. "Usually that process would take place over a geological time span, far too long to worry us. But they believe that in this instance it will happen relatively rapidly. Of course, we can't be certain. I'm not an expert, but it looks like a reasonable conclusion to me, from what data I've seen. Nevertheless, we'll want to continue to collect more information, and have it all reviewed by anyone who's interested." She gave Paul a small nod. She wanted his opinion for sure, but everyone in the community should have the opportunity.

Once again Caroline steered things in the direction they'd decided. "But even if they're right about this, people do live in swamps, don't they?"

Verity nodded and looked at Jeffrey. "Of course they do. But we didn't build this place for a swamp —others will have to explain the exact requirements for constructing dwellings suited to such a different environment, but it will require us to rebuild or extensively remodel the whole compound. Which will mean a lot of work. And before we begin repairs on our existing buildings, we should plan out the renovations we'll want to make. Then do all the work at the same time. Because it will be a massive endeavor, and the time we have to complete it may be limited, we'll need to start soon. If we decide to do the work at all."

"It would be a huge undertaking"—that was Fox finally contributing again—"so we certainly ought to start in on the work as soon as possible. As soon as we've decided precisely what needs to be done. But it sounds necessary. If that assessment proves correct, and we should start making plans in case it is." He leaned forward and pinned her with a hard gaze as he continued. "But other than the experts ending up with egg on their face because they got it wrong, why *wouldn't* we decide to press forward?"

Verity nodded. "Because there's another option available to us. We could move."

"Move? Move where? Assuming we could find a large abandoned farm or something capable of supporting our entire community, we'd still have to do a lot of work to make it livable. And that's aside from any special requirements for living in a swamp."

Thankfully Tracy added her two cents. "I really don't like the idea of living in a swamp."

"I don't think any of us are especially enthused. It would mean a very different way of life, after all." Verity pursed her lips in distaste. "The cars, electric carts, the roads and walkways would all be useless."

She met the eyes of the other councilors. "Probably have to get around the compound in boats or something. I certainly don't fancy swimming. Not only a different way of life but one of considerably reduced standards compared to what we're used to."

Jeffery nodded, but what he said then was, "We could and would adapt. We'd survive, perhaps even thrive, and that's what's important."

"Is it?" Caroline stepped into the conversation. "My husband conceived and created the FURC project to do more than survive the collapse of civilization. Our purpose is to rebuild society, to remake it better than it was. To do that we need to more than just survive. Or even thrive, in what sounds quite a backward way of life. We need to excel, to grow and continue to improve and innovate. But how can we do that in a swamp?"

Alvin Fox snorted, then looked embarrassed. "I don't see how we could do that by moving, either."

Caroline looked to Verity, who still stood. Running her gaze around the room again, she gave them a small smile. "There are three possibilities. While we had not begun building the Northeast FURC before everything fell apart, the Midwest complex was mostly finished, and there was only a skeleton staff. Some administrators, and the contractors completing the construction. And of course the external security personnel. But that leaves plenty of room for our entire community. And, more importantly, the infrastructure to replicate what we've got here."

Paul nodded in appreciation of the point. "But, based on what we know of the effects of the meteorite impact, Southern Illinois may have been hit just as hard by the quake as us." He paused. "Though I don't suppose they're in any danger of turning into a swamp, it would be a long and difficult move, to get our entire community there. To then have to repair those buildings and finish any incomplete construction..."

"It would be a challenge. But then every choice we face will mean extreme difficulties." Verity took a deep breath. "There's also the Northwest FURC to consider. A much longer walk—"

"Walk!" Tracy's eyes boggled. "Surely we'd not have to walk across the whole country. Or even the shorter trek to the Midwest."

"Of course we'd have to walk." Verity shook her head. "We don't have enough cars and carts to carry everyone, much less all we'd want to take with us on the journey. Those vehicles would have to be reserved for the injured. But mostly they'd be used to haul the equipment, the food, the resources we will bring along." She smiled wider. "So much walking, it'll be good for us."

Caroline got them back on track. "You said the Northwest FURC was an option?"

"Yes. That complex was completed and ready to go online." Whatever had gone wrong there, it definitely wasn't because they weren't prepared. "They were fully staffed and should only be lacking the so-called FedU students, but it's a far larger compound and ought to be able to accommodate all of us."

Caroline nodded. "You said there are three options—what's the third?"

"The Southwest FURC has also been finished. I was able to contact the team there earlier today and confirm they're ready. They've had no disasters and only the construction crew and a handful of administrators are there. So there's plenty of room." And it was quite a different sort of place, but they didn't want to talk about that. Yet.

Verity continued. "So we have hard choices we need to make, and unfortunately we'll have to make those decisions quickly. If we choose to move, we'll need to get going as soon as possible—the longer we wait, the more conditions will deteriorate and make traveling more difficult. Or rebuilding, if we choose that path. Either way, we don't have much time for discussion."

Chapter 27

Difficult Decisions

5:55 p.m. Saturday, May 28th
The Community Council Conference Room

CAROLINE STRODE INTO the chamber a few minutes early to find all the other councilors seated and ready for what would surely be the most crucial session yet. There had been a flurry of activity over the past seven hours, a lot of investigation and asking questions. Of answers and arguments.

They'd continued to collect as much data as the situation allowed, and everyone in the FURC with a sufficient background to understand the issues this involved—and that was an awful lot of people here—had gone over the information and tested their conclusions as far as possible. And they all agreed that the basic premise Verity had presented was correct.

That didn't mean it *was* right—consensus was nothing like proof—but nobody was willing to wager the future on the possibility that everyone was wrong.

They didn't agree on how long it would take for the entire area to turn into swampland. But the unknown timescale involved only made it seem urgent to decide on a course of action and start working on it. And there was no argument about what the basic options were. Only which of the two to choose.

Moving close to ten thousand people thousands of miles, most of them walking, with all the baggage they'd be taking, was a daunting prospect, and most seemed opposed to the idea. The question of where they would go wasn't being discussed. Staying here certainly sounded a safer, easier choice, and the hypothetical deterioration of their quality of life in the possibly distant future hardly worth worrying over. Basically building a new complex inside the existing walls would be a lot of work, but it could be accomplished piecemeal. And this was their home.

Caroline certainly had her work cut out for her. Verity was on her side, but the woman was not persuasive. Articulate, but she hadn't learned the skills needed to sway opinion. The rest of the councilors, they had spent a lot of this day talking to the people they represented, explaining and listening. Finding out where people stood. Caroline had been planting seeds and laying the groundwork for this meeting.

Rounding the room, then taking the chair at the head of the table, she took a minute to compose her thoughts as the muted discussions among the other councilors trailed off into silence. "One minute until the six o'clock time we agreed upon and we're all here, so I'm calling the session to order. Everybody in the community has presumably watched the earlier meeting and learned the details of the situation we're dealing with and the decision we're facing, so I'll try to avoid boring you by repeating what everyone should know. Whatever choice we make today, and I believe we're all on the same page in thinking we need to make it right away, there will still be lots of planning and more detailed decisions to make."

She paused and looked around, to see if anyone intended to interrupt. "But those can wait. First we need to choose between two starkly different paths. Do we stay or do we go?"

Paul jumped in with the first comment. "While I understand wanting to address that huge question first, to figure out what the best answer is I think we have to know more about what either option would entail."

Nodding, Caroline turned to face Alvin and Jeffrey. "I know you two have spent a lot of time today consulting the various contractors and architects to discover more about what we'd have to do, were we to remain here. Could you address Paul's question, explain to him and everyone watching on their pads what that would look like?"

Jeffrey nodded at Alvin, who then turned to address her. "While the quake did its share of damage and collapsed several smaller structures, most of the buildings are still sound. Except for the ones extensively damaged by last night's fires. However, we're already seeing substantial subsidence in some areas of the compound, undermining some foundations." He closed his eyes a moment and sighed, then gave her a somber stare. "We'd want to rebuild all those first, but eventually—and sooner, rather than later—we would have to basically rebuild everything, a new and different complex, with structures on stilt foundations to stand up out of the water. And even then sinkholes could bring down even the largest."

Councilor Minchin continued from there. "And as Acting Director Belue remarked, we'd need boats for navigating around the compound. Not yet. Not for a while, but it won't be that long before the carts become useless. Then we'll have to rely on the larger vehicles, the trucks, to traverse the complex until it turns 'swampy' enough for boats. And then there is the wall." He shrugged. "We can make repairs to it now, but in time maintaining it will become—let's call it impractical. The sonic wards won't last, while the fence won't be much of a defense either. Meaning we'd have to worry about gators and snakes."

Alvin picked up on that. "It's doubtful we'd face any real threat from human invaders in such an environment, but you see there'd be other dangers."

Caroline nodded. Hopefully everyone was paying attention and starting to realize staying wasn't a 'safe and easy' choice. "Thank you for that succinct report. Now,"—she turned to look at first Paul then Verity—"I believe you two have been studying what would be involved in moving the community across the country."

Verity began. "Of course we have the carts, and most of the vehicles here are hybrids. We'd have to convert those that aren't. We'd also have to build a mobile charging station powered by a wireless node to recharge those batteries. Those would be some of the larger jobs we'd have to do if we moved."

"Wirelessly? You're saying we'd be able to take our power supply and the transmission system with us when we left?"

She gestured at Paul, who spoke to that specific question. "The power techs and I have been looking at how to make our power system mobile. It would take a lot of work, but we believe it's feasible. Preferable, if we do decide to move, because availability of energy on the outside is likely to be...lacking."

Verity continued. "We could use the ambulances as mobile clinics. We have a few transport trucks and lots of pickups, enough to carry all the essential equipment and supplies we'd need to take, but we'd have to limit the amount of personal luggage hauled —with anything above that to be carried by the person who deems the extra worth the effort. The carts would be useful for those who still have mobility issues because of quake-related injuries. Or who just get tired."

Dr. Harker spoke to that. "Even the most critically injured are healing fast, so there won't be a lot of need for that. And all but the newest newcomers to receive the Lift Virus have developed strong constitutions. Walking twenty miles a day, with breaks —well, most of us won't have much trouble managing that. Though we may grumble." Apparently the woman had a sense of humor. Caroline hadn't had a chance to spend much time around her, as the good doctor avoided the council meetings as much as she could get away with. That would have to change.

Verity nodded. "The guards could travel on the outskirts of the main group, to warn of approaching threats, and scout ahead to find the safest and easiest route forward. So twenty miles a day would be a reasonable goal. It would still take us a few months to get wherever we go, barring any unforeseen difficulties, but we'd have power, and the FURCSnet servers are mobile. So we'd still be able to use our pads to stay connected." Which would be vital. With ten thousand people on the march, the leading edge and back end of that procession would be separated by a long distance. And the security officers and guards would need to be in constant touch.

Caroline smiled at Verity. “Thank you, Director Belue.” The woman had managed to make the long slog sound almost civilized. Hopefully everyone saw moving as the more appealing option now.

Nodding again, Verity had more to say. “There is the issue of gas—we have only a small reserve, so we’ll have to scavenge along the way. And hygiene, that may be a problem, as we won’t be able to bring showers with us. We could take some tubs, I think. But we’ll have to rely on whatever water or cleaning facilities we can find as we travel. Laundry will be a challenge as well.” Great, it wasn’t sounding so civilized anymore. “But at least we won’t have to worry about drinking water.”

Caroline needed to stop the bleeding. “Alright, I think we’ve answered the question in general terms —what either choice would involve, what those two decisions would lead to. So unless any of you have a follow-up question…” She gave them a minute, but while they all appeared deep in thought, none of the other councilors asked anything. Not that they had any more ‘answers’.

“Then I’ll go ahead and call for a vote. It’s clear we need to make a decision as soon as possible, and we’re not likely to know much more about what the potential consequences of our choice will be, before it's too late anyway. So I make a motion that we begin preparations and move this community as soon as we're ready. Will anyone second the motion?"

She held her breath as the others looked to each other, considering. Verity would vote with her. But she had asked the woman to wait. Because it would be better if someone else seconded the motion. After a moment that seemed to keep stretching so she felt sure Verity would have to jump in, Paul nodded and raised his hand. "I second it. I'll be involved in a lot of the most difficult preparations, but the challenge excites me. And I'd rather work for the better future than just strive to survive."

Dr. Harker laughed. "Our DNA is changing and improving. Certainly we should try to advance as a community as well. Otherwise we would be throwing away a glorious gift." That made three votes for moving. Verity's one more would mean a majority, but Caroline hoped for a greater consensus, to rally people behind the decision.

Alvin Fox leaned forward and met her eye. "I'll support moving too. It seems the best thing for the good of the community. And 'home' is wherever we are, together. This, clearly, is no longer the best *location* for us, so we go and settle in a better place."

Verity nodded. "I agree. We should start making plans now." Five votes. It had passed handily.

Only, two councilors hadn't had their say yet, so Caroline shook her head. "Let's hear from Councilors Minchin and Johnson first." She smiled at Jeffrey and Tracy. "Even if you oppose the motion, it's important for your voice to be heard."

Tracy looked around the table. "Neither option sounds good, and I doubt the teachers or other university staff have any particular preference between the two, so I suppose we'll be happy to go along with what the community as a whole want."

Jeffrey shrugged. "Personally, I'd rather move. It's not like a swamp offers a lot of options for landscaping, and I'd prefer not to witness the deterioration of the Green and the beautiful parks and lawns we have now. And I'm not sure how well milk cows and swamps mix, so I imagine the Ag workers want to go as well. But I'm afraid the majority of workers here would rather stay. Lots of rebuilding and new construction doesn't daunt them—I think they were looking forward to all that work—and I think *Acting* Director Belue underestimates what a comfortable, advanced complex we could create if we remained." He shrugged again. "But it seems I'm outvoted."

Caroline appreciated how well he had threaded that needle, expressing the opinions of those who'd oppose the move so they felt represented, but making it sound as if losing wasn't such a big deal. "The motion carries, six to one, then."

She glanced at Verity. "Acting Director Belue is clearly anxious to start planning our move, and she can begin those preparations if she wishes. However, we all had a rough night last night and a difficult day today, and some of us have other work to attend to. So I move we adjourn until this time tomorrow. Then we can hear her provisional plans and suggest any alterations we think necessary.

"Tomorrow being Sunday, I think we should all spend the day in prayer and contemplation. Before beginning the hard work Monday morning."

The motion carried by voice vote. Verity rushed out, no doubt to start preparing things—apparently her son hadn't shared his own plans. The others all filed out after her, with a little less haste, but eager, except for Dr. Harker who stayed behind. But Caroline didn't want to talk to her in front of the viewing public.

Out in the hall, though. "Are you sure you want to go through with this, Amita? Everything's so unsettled now..."

The woman shook her head. "I won't give him a chance to change his mind."

"Well, then. You need to begin attending council sessions regularly and taking them seriously. My husband was mentoring David, not only with regard to the law but with an eye toward him taking Miles' place as director someday."

Amita blinked, and from her expression had no clue where Caroline was going with this. So she explained. "He's too young and inexperienced for the position now, but you can help him. By making the most of your own leadership role. You accepted the responsibility already. So step up." And the doctor would make a valuable ally for Caroline meanwhile. "You're about to marry the man who's probably going to be the FURC's top executive one day."

"Good." The woman nodded as if to herself. "I think he's capable. Not ambitious—which is likely a good thing for a leader—but it does mean I will need to encourage him." She squinted at Caroline. "And if it also means I have to cut back on my research to spend more time in council meetings, so be it."

They were approaching the First Councilor's office then and saw David waiting in the corridor outside. Their conversation ended there. But Caroline had already said what she'd needed to, and the other woman had understood.

Inside, she sat behind her desk and stared over it at the couple now standing before her. "I assume you haven't told your mother yet, David?"

The young man shook his head, then smiled. "I thought it better to present her with a *fait accompli* to avoid any delays. It's not like we have much time to get this done." Better if she was here for this, for several reasons, but it was his decision.

Caroline shook her head. “You two won’t have a lot of time for your honeymoon either. Are you sure you want to commit yourselves to a life together?”

“I am.” Amita set her jaw in determination. “It has taken too long to get here, but I won’t turn back now.”

David gave his bride-to-be a fond look. “Yes, I’m sure too.”

“Well then, I pronounce you man and wife. You may kiss the bride while I log your marriage.” Caroline wasn’t sure she approved, personally, but there was no cause for her to officially object to the union—and after bending her head to the pad to officially record it, to give them the illusion of a little privacy, she looked up through her lashes and watched them kiss. And decided she did approve after all.

Epilogue

Future Action

7:05 a.m. Monday, May 30th
First floor of the Medical Center

TIM MACTIERNEY SAT beside the chief's bed and listened to the low angry rumble escaping from the man as he adjusted the pillows propping him up and tried to keep from cursing in front of the sisters bustling about the small recovery ward. Once Cameron had settled down, Tim had to ask. "You wanted me to come, Chief. So spit it out." On-duty he'd never have been so informal, but he'd been off for a good half hour and wanted some rest himself.

"They won't let me drive." The man had to have seen the confusion on Tim's face. And after a pause he elaborated. "I could get up and walk right now—not run, but then I've never liked running, got more than enough of that in the army—but they won't let me. Not without assistance, until the physical therapist certifies I won't collapse or something."

Tim nodded. "Glad to hear you're recovering so fast, sir. Did you want me to accompany you somewhere in particular?"

"Not now, boy. But later, since I can't drive for a while. I'm making my truck"—Tim was acquainted with the huge, gleaming white monster with a king-sized cab—"the mobile command for the Guards, so I'll need a driver." Ah.

Well, after their performance in the wake of the quake, the chief had promoted his daughter Grace, as well as Lacey Peterson—they were both sergeants now, which made too many with rank for the supervisory positions available. Coincidentally, a new job had been created, chief's driver, and Tim had clearly been chosen for it. Though he imagined he would be working as executive assistant and general dogsbody as well. "I'm to be your driver, then?"

"Yes. Well. I'm sure you understand it was difficult to decide who would replace Lieutenant Miles as my deputy, and I did consider you for that, but in the end I chose to promote Steve Rose."

Tim nodded. "I think he *is* the best man for the job, sir." It had been awkward when Grace became a guard, and he'd been happy to hear of her promotion, to know he didn't outrank her anymore. Being promoted to lieutenant would've been problematic. And it wasn't as if he was ambitious. "And I'm happy...I'd be honored, sir, to be your chauffeur."

Spending lots of time close to the man he hoped would someday be his father-in-law would be good. If it didn't get him killed.

8:55 a.m. Monday, May 30th
Security Chief's Office, Security HQ

SUSAN STOOD BEFORE the desk and thought again how much more suited Bob Kirkland seemed, to the position of Security Chief, than Anthony Nelson had. Their former boss had always been more a lone wolf than a leader, though he had been a great teacher. But Bob had spent decades as sheriff, running a law enforcement office. And by all accounts, he'd done a good job.

More importantly, Kirkland's promotion meant someone had to fill his old position as Deputy Chief —Susan hoped getting called in this morning meant she was about to be offered the job. She'd lamented the lack of opportunity for advancement in Security often, and even considered resigning, trying to start her own business. Had largely decided on a private security firm as her best option.

But the move put paid to that idea. In the short term, anyway, until they'd settled somewhere else—so at least as far as the near future went, her opportunities were extremely limited. "You wanted to see me, Chief Kirkland?"

"I expect you've already guessed—I want you to be Deputy Chief." The man looked like a rough and ready version of Santa Claus, but his tone was typically genial. "Do you want the job?"

"Certainly, sir. But if I may ask—why not Rawlings? He's got decades of experience as a deputy in a sheriff's office, and choosing him would please the people who came from Charlesberg."

Bob snorted. "I don't make decisions or choose who to put in positions to 'send signals'. And those folks have been here three years. They've fully integrated by now and don't need any special treatment—the more recent newcomers are a motley lot without a common identity, so if they haven't assimilated yet, they soon will. Now, Rawlings is a good senior officer. So are Courdray and Salazar. But you're better suited to being my deputy."

That was what she thought too, having analyzed her competition. "And I accept the job, sir."

"Good. And I'd have wanted to pick you even if Nelson hadn't suggested it. Now, you know the job is mostly administrative—I'll want you running this place, basically—or wherever we're operating out of in transit—while I mosey around keeping an eye on things and staying in touch with the community."

"Yes, sir." And that was exactly what she wanted to be doing, what he should be doing. And when they eventually got wherever they went, she'd be in a good position to set up her own operation.

9:40 a.m. Monday, May 30th
FURC Director's Office, Administration Building

PAUL STEPPED IN and Verity lifted her head to peer at him. Pushing aside her workpad, she sat up straighter and addressed him. "Close the door, this discussion needs to be private."

Shutting the door behind him cut off the incessant buzzing of frenetic activity he'd passed through in the outer office. Preparations for the move were in full swing, and the fifth floor of Admin remained the hub of coordination for everything. "I presume it's something important to pull me away from what I was working on." Her summons had reached him down in the transmission room, helping some techs figure out how to make the power system mobile.

"It's related to that, actually." And she frowned at him. "You've shown yourself to be very responsible, Paul. As a councilor, and there won't be another election for a long time, so you'll continue in that role indefinitely." She wasn't saying anything other than what he already knew, and she wasn't one who felt the need to encourage people. And he didn't see how this could have anything to do with his work on the power system. "And you were very helpful, getting the power supply back online and repairing the transmission system."

Paul nodded. "Somebody had to jump in, and I happened to be there and know enough to help out. It was good experience for me."

"Yes. And you're now a doctoral student in theoretical physics. All of that is why I have decided to confide in you." He waited for her to continue. "I'd have to tell someone, since with Miles gone I'm now the only one who knows—the nature of our 'experimental' power supply."

Paul smiled. "The sphere. I had wondered. It's obviously classified information." And far more restricted than he would've guessed.

Verity nodded again. "Inside that container is a microscopic black hole."

Whistling, he thought about that. "Theoretically, that's always been considered possible." A black hole on such a tiny scale, pulverizing infinitesimally minute matter, would—so they believed—generate a massive amount of energy. "But in practical terms, building such a device is thought to be impossible."

He shook his head. “A lot like time travel, the math may make perfect sense, but nobody has ever found a way to actually do it.”

She cocked her head and studied him for a long moment. “Yes, well. That’s what our power supply *is.* And it would be a good idea if someone who had an idea how it worked knew that. Particularly if the person was also working directly with it. And such a person might want to start studying the technology to determine what problems it might pose down the road.”

Paul frowned. “Yes, indeed.” As exciting as this information was, the revelation of what he had been handling was also terribly frightening. It was daunting to consider the responsibility she’d just handed him. But it was also an amazing opportunity.

1:25 p.m. Monday, May 30th
The second floor of Security HQ

SARA STOOD IDLY in the hall, looking through the door to what used to be the chief’s private quarters and watching as Anthony Nelson rooted around in a drawer. Finally he straightened, shoving something into his jacket pocket as he turned. Grinning, he started toward her. “Feels good, being back, I’m sure. You've even got your uniform on." And officers didn't usually wear them, except for certain ceremonial functions. But she was still a trainee, again rather, and wanted to show everyone she was Security once more. Even if her status remained probationary. For now.

"I'm grateful you gave me the chance to turn my life around, Chief." Backing out of his way, she rued the fact that she wouldn't be going with him. But if he could only take one person along, of course that would be his wife. And though Sara couldn't escape her own past, it would be nice to be out from under the shadow of Kat and how awesome she was.

Nelson shook his head. "Not chief anymore, or ever again if I have my way. And I did *not* give you a chance to turn your life around, Ms. King. You were already doing that before I even knew. I just recognized what was happening, acknowledged it."

She shrugged. If he couldn't accept her thanks, that didn't change how she felt. "What had you forgotten, sir?" She inclined her head at his pocket.

"Oh, just a little gadget I got a long time ago and thought might be useful where I'm going." He trotted down the steps, speaking back over his shoulder at her. "Don't worry about me. Just focus on turning yourself into an impressive officer."

"As you say, sir." And she would.

7:10 p.m. Monday, May 30th
The Belue residence

DAVID TOOK TWO more books from one of the shelves in the room he'd kept at his mother's house —he was saving Sara Woods' Antony Maitland mysteries but leaving the Perry Mason books behind, as well as his John Grisham novels. Not based on how much he liked them, but on what was allowed. The books already available as electronic editions on the net had to be abandoned, because there was only so much room. And he didn't want to keep those hard copies enough to carry them in a backpack.

His mother had granted permission though, for any books not held in digital form in the FURCSnet to be included in the mountains of luggage that they would load on the trucks. And his Sara Woods were unusual in only existing in physical form. Might be the only copies left anywhere for all he knew. These legal mysteries and courtroom thrillers, which he'd started reading as a boy, were what had inspired him to study law. Though there wasn't all that much legal content to the stories.

Still, he wanted to be able to reread his favorite novels whatever the future might hold, or wherever they went. And especially on what everyone was already calling The Long Slog—when they hadn't even started their journey yet.

He shook his head. Wait to call it that—it likely would be a long slog indeed—at the end, presuming they actually got where they were going someday. It would be better to start with a smile, full of hope, as the trip would probably wear them down over time. And *he* had *no* call to let himself feel gloomy.

Saturday night he'd gone back to Amita's house as her husband, and they'd both been given this day off as part of a truncated honeymoon. He'd go back there soon, after leaving these books boxed up for a worker to collect in the morning. He wasn't bothering to move into Amita's properly—preparations for moving everyone out were proceeding apace, and it looked like they'd all be leaving here before the end of the week. Then, for many months, none of them would have a house. At night they'd have to sleep in tents or vehicles or whatever shelter they happened to find that was fit for human habitation. He didn't expect to discover much of that, or anywhere they'd be particularly safe. But protecting the community would be honorable work.

After three years on the job, he was now at least competent at it, and he hoped to eventually become as capable as Lt. Miles.

9:35 p.m. Monday, May 30th
The middle of the Green

KAT THREW HER pack up into the basket, then turned to give her mom a hug. Neither of them had been given much time to grieve before now, but the separate journeys they were taking would afford all too much opportunity to think about their loss. On the other hand, they might be too busy staying alive to wallow much.

Caroline smiled and stepped back. There was a small gathering to see Kat and Tony off—they'd said most of their goodbyes earlier, throughout that day in between packing and preparing for this trip. She was pleased her mother had taken the time to show up, considering how busy the woman was. Tim had driven Chief Cameron here in a cart, and Ken sat in the passenger seat scowling—he'd already expressed his extreme displeasure at losing her in a more voluble manner. A serious-looking Verity had come too —surprising, since the still 'acting' director had lots to do.

Tony was already in the gondola, watching as a fan finished filling the balloon's envelope. The couple had spent several hours this afternoon getting a crash course in operating a hot-air balloon—though why the FURC even had this remained a mystery to her—because they had to leave soon, and the winds were unusually calm this evening. One thing they'd learned was how dangerous taking off—and landing—could be. Obstacles near the surface of the earth, like buildings and trees, caused fluctuations such as wind shear and cross-currents that could wreck the craft. So they had to launch while the winds stayed relatively still.

She watched Tony fire up the burners to slowly start warming the air in the envelope and placed an arm over the side of the basket. Just in case.

Then Verity approached and addressed her. "It seems likely we'll find ourselves a new home, either at the Midwest or Southwest FURC compound, and if we do you can join us there." Lowering her voice, she continued. "More importantly, you need to find out what's been going on at the Northwest facility—something is very wrong there—and fix it. I'm sorry I can't tell you any more than that."

"I thought our task was just to reestablish communications and evaluate the compound's suitability for taking us all in, should the other compounds prove inhospitable." Kat glanced over her shoulder at Tony.

Verity shook her head. "He doesn't know. I decided to leave it to you to inform him about the true nature of your mission." Well, that certainly made a pleasant change from the past. The woman stepped back and raised her voice again. "Take care. Brave heart. And God be with you."

Kat felt the edge of the basket starting to lift her arm and climbed over into the gondola. She let her husband adjust the burners as they gently rose from the ground while she waved at the people they were leaving behind. Looked down at them and—as they ascended higher—the circular landscape of the park they called the Green, then the Admin building and other familiar structures. Familiar but strange from this perspective. The place that had been her home for almost five years.

But she wouldn't be coming back. None of them would ever return, which should make her sad. But instead she felt thrilled.

As it all dwindled to tiny specks below, lit up by the glow of the scattered lights, she breathed deeply and embraced a sense of adventure. The journey itself promised plenty of excitement.

She and Tony would take turns flying this thing —the only way to steer it was by adjusting the burners to heat or cool the air in the envelope and cause the balloon to rise or fall in altitude. The wind blew in different directions at different elevations. Their altitude would also determine their speed.

While they had a special laptop that could communicate with the weather satellites to obtain *some* information about wind speed and direction at various elevations—and about possible storms, another potential danger—they'd mostly be flying by feel.

The trip might take a week. Or two. Depending on how fast they flew—and how roundabout a route they ended up having to take to get there, assuming they actually arrived at their destination. They had oxygen on board in case they needed it. They didn't plan to fly higher than twelve thousand feet, even to go over the Rockies, but they didn't know what was waiting for them along their journey.

Anything could happen. They hoped to fly high enough to avoid unfriendly eyes—they certainly did not want anyone taking potshots at them. And they would try to keep their speed as fast as seemed safe —this gondola which would be their home was efficiently designed and sturdy enough, but it was also small and uncomfortable. The sooner they reached their goal, the better.

They also hoped to avoid landing along the way —stopping would not only delay their arrival, but it would be difficult and potentially dangerous to land anywhere, as would taking off again. But problems of one kind or another could force them down. One way or another, they'd get where they were headed, even if they didn't end up flying all the way.

Finally they rose to where the wind was blowing west-northwest—at about fifteen miles an hour, but she didn't feel the slightest breeze.

Tony turned down the burner to keep them from rising higher, then gave her a warm smile. “Should take us out over the Gulf soon.”

Kat moved closer, and he took her in his arms—for a while, at least, he wouldn’t need his hands. To pilot the balloon, anyway. Unfortunately it required constant attention and monitoring, so they couldn’t let themselves get too distracted. But she’d wanted more time alone with her husband, and she was going to get that.

She’d also wished for excitement and adventure and would be getting plenty of that. On this trip for a start. And then it sounded as if things might turn really interesting once they got where they were going. She intended to enjoy every moment.

About the Author

JAMES LITHERLAND is a graduate of the University of South Florida who currently resides as a Virtual Hermit in the wilds of West Tennessee.

He's lived in various places and done a number of jobs—he has been an office worker and done hard manual labor, worked (briefly) in the retail and service sectors, and he's been an instructor. Through all that, he's always been a writer.

He is a Christian who tries to walk the walk (and not talk much.)

Lightning Source UK Ltd.
Milton Keynes UK
UKHW011856161220
375343UK00001B/95